Ruffled Feathers

BY THE SAME AUTHOR

Artist, Undone
Virgin Gingelly
The Third Squad
A Tamil Month

RUFFLED FEATHERS

Stories

V. SANJAY KUMAR

BLOOMSBURY
NEW DELHI • LONDON • OXFORD • NEW YORK • SYDNEY

BLOOMSBURY INDIA
Bloomsbury Publishing India Pvt. Ltd
Second Floor, LSC Building No. 4, DDA Complex, Pocket C – 6 & 7,
Vasant Kunj, New Delhi, 110070

BLOOMSBURY, BLOOMSBURY INDIA and the Diana logo
are trademarks of Bloomsbury Publishing Plc

First published in India 2022
This edition published 2022

ISBN: PB: 978-93-54351-13-6; eBook: 978-93-54351-21-1

2 4 6 8 10 9 7 5 3 1

Typeset in Sabon LT Std by Manipal Technologies Limited
Printed and bound in India by Thomson Press India Ltd.

MIX
Paper from
responsible sources
FSC® C010615

CONTENTS

The Forecaddie

'Will you ever buy a house?' asked his friend Mano.

Yuva saw stars. 'No,' he said.

'There is one for sale—cheap. My neighbour, the driver, needs money for an operation.'

Yuva thought about it. 'How much? Actually, don't tell me. I might kill someone. Or sell a kidney.'

'Nobody will buy your kidney,' said Mano.

'We will see. How much?'

'Ten lakh. Cash. It has a toilet.'

A private toilet was worth something. 'I don't have the money,' said Yuva. 'I have never seen ten lakh rupees in my life.'

'Why don't you rob a bank?' said Mano.

Yuva thought about it. There was a big bank next to the jewellery store. People came in Mercedes cars and bought diamond necklaces for ₹2–3 lakh. Cash. Every day the store sent sackfuls of notes to that bank. Yuva imagined the heist. The guard would be seated outside with his big antique rifle. There would be a few customers, old men and women who still visited the bank. And some middle-class wimps who served as bank officers. All Mano and Yuva had to do was wear masks, knock the guard down and threaten people. Nobody inside would be brave enough to resist.

His stomach made a noise. When things were really quiet, Yuva could hear it. It had a mind of its own, and near McRennett's pastry shop, it growled. The smell of fresh baking came through the door. His insides contracted.

A man walked past carrying hot buns in a brown paper bag, the butter stains showing.

'Go in first,' he told Mano. 'I will follow.'

He walked in behind him. The place was cool, and the smell was heavenly. Yuva asked the salesgirl the price of a few items. He pretended he couldn't make up his mind. Mano hated this charade. He pulled at Yuva's sleeve. 'Let's go, machan,' he said. The salesgirl smiled at Yuva. She reached into the counter, pulled out a fresh cream pastry and offered it to him. 'Take it,' she said. It was soft and it had a white creamy layer on which were two juicy pieces of pineapple and one red cherry. His stomach lurched as he held it. Outside, he took a big bite and gave the rest to his friend. The fresh cream melted in his mouth. The pineapple had been dipped in sugar syrup. He licked his lips.

How did she know? How did she guess he had no money? Was it obvious?

'She likes me,' he told Mano.

'Machan,' said Mano, 'you look hungry.'

'She felt sorry for me?'

'Yes,' said Mano. 'You are lucky you look hungry.'

He felt hungry all the time. His mother said it was because he was growing. He knew it wasn't just about food.

The first time they stole, it was a packet of chips from a store. Yuva refused to open it. The next day he wanted to return it. 'Don't,' said Mano. A day later the packet was still there. They ripped it open and ate the chips, one by one. 'You shouldn't think so much,' said Mano. Yuva stopped thinking. He flicked pencils and pens in the Corporation School. He left his old slippers outside a temple and wore someone else's. He stole savouries as he walked past street vendors and burnt his fingers once. A couple of times he had to run. He was fast and he knew the city well. Once, he ducked into a house while being chased and in a split second he straightened, walked slowly up to the door, picked up a milk packet from the floor, bit its corner, drank it and left.

'We have to stop looking like rowdies,' said Mano. 'Otherwise, we will get caught. The police will take one look at us and put us in the lock-up.'

'How?' asked Yuva. 'Should we steal some clothes?'

'Look at yourself,' said Mano. They stood beside a car, bent and looked at themselves in the side mirror.

'What's wrong?'

'Your face is pinched, your cheeks are hollow and your eyes.'

'What about my eyes?'

'You look like you just ran away from a Home.'

Yuva used his fingers to brush and flatten his hair. He widened his eyes and stuck his tongue out. 'What should we do?'

'Eat properly for ten days. Our look will improve.'

A week later they went to a pavement shop, the kind that popped up unexpectedly and shut before the constabulary arrived. The vendor spread his wares, set up a board that declared a cut-price, and a crowd gathered in no time. Yuva picked up a showy shirt. 'No,' said Mano.

'Not that belt,' said his friend. Yuva put back the shiny belt.

'Here, wear these glasses.' They had clear lenses. 'Glasses make you look honest,' said Mano.

'Why?'

'Because thieves don't wear spectacles.'

That evening they wore their new clothes and went mad.

'Gana, gana, gana,' shouted Mano, shaking his hips. He was twisting into a rope, and he was leaping the length of the room. The Tamil song was on speaker and it went thud, thud, thud. 'Yuvan Shankar Raja,' said Mano, shouting out the name of their favourite music composer. Yuva got started. He could dance. Parts of his body that did nothing for a week came alive. He shifted from toe to toe and soon his hands were moving, his eyes slanted, his knee bent stylishly.

'Thalaiva,' shouted Mano, 'what a pose!'

Yuva pumped his shoulders, fluidly skated to the wall and halted. 'Dai Michael,' he yelled, turned once, twice and twirled the hat on his head. Thump, thump, thump.

'Go, go, go,' said his friend.

They had been drinking. Yuva danced harder, beating himself with his hands, throwing his head from side to side. He saw stars. The music kept playing and he couldn't stop. He was sweating profusely, and he felt thirsty. He drank more beer. The angels came, soft, white and fluffy. They settled into his arms. 'Machan, can you see them?' he said. The song slowed; the beat petered out. A ballad began to a slow rhythm. His horny friend hugged him, thrusting his bony hips into Yuva's back. They fell on their backs, exhausted.

Yuva remembered his first possessions. His first golf ball had no maker's name because it had been erased by use. It was egg-shell white many months ago, now its colour was mud. His first golf club was a broken five iron that he had repaired. Its grip was hard, and his fingers had blisters for a month.

The Gymkhana was his home course. He had grown up in it as a forecaddie. During practice sessions, players stood in a line and teed off, shouting fore. Yuva and his young friends ran holding their heads, picked up the balls and placed them in buckets. He liked going on rounds as a forecaddie. The Gymkhana was a links course with evil rough, tall, unkempt grass where balls could easily get lost. Yuva stood a hundred yards ahead of the players and tracked where the ball went. Golfers employed a forecaddie because the cost was lower than the cost of a new golf ball. A lost ball also meant a penalty, and on occasion a penalty meant a lost bet.

Yuva had started at the age of five. He ran fast during practice and kept his eyes peeled. If a ball went missing, he got cuffed behind the ear by the caddie master. Those days he had one proper pair of shorts tied to his waist by a thin rope. He had a T-shirt that was big for him. All his shirts were bigger than him till he was in his teens. They wore sponsor logos and were made of synthetic material. They were hand-me-downs from players.

Some afternoons, in summer, the course was empty, and no one was around to stop him and his three friends from entering the place. They carried a club each and some old balls. He had his trusty five iron. He played the entire course with one club, putting with it as well. He learnt the game without caring for style or technique. He had an athletic, free-flowing swing. His ball flight was long, and he could chip the ball in ten different ways. He learnt how to read greens. The big slope and the small slopes. The grain of the grass. The way it had been cut.

His father was a senior caddie. He would mimic the players he had caddied for. He would mimic their English. 'Golf teaches you how to be honest,' he said, with a straight face. He would laugh uproariously and then very solemnly he would say in Tamil, 'But God teaches you how to make a living.'

Yuva learnt to help out players. He learnt how to improve the lie of the ball so that it could be hit better. He could do this with his feet. His toes curled around the ball and moved it. He would place the ball on a tuft of grass or a patch of upraised soil. In the tall grass called rough, he learnt how to shift the ball into shorter grass. He would pretend to search even after finding the ball. He would place the ball where it could be hit easily, move away, then come back and shout as if he had just found it. He learnt to walk with the ball in his toes. He walked many a yard with it, and old players began to brag about how long they were hitting the ball. With him as the caddie, the members scored better. He received fat tips.

His mother was extremely unhappy when he followed his father to the golf course. She shouted at both of them.

'Don't you have any dreams?' she asked Yuva.

'Only dreams,' he said.

He was so young nothing could be better than going with his old man to this huge, open playground where he could run around on green grass with his friends, and occasionally play a game for free.

'Your son will become a jobless drunk, just like you,' shouted his mother. Old Man stood in the doorway, his cap in his hand, his teeth showing. He had a wicked grin. He was past caring about anything, least of all his son. His wife hated that he was on retainer because it made him lazy and he carried the bag just three times a week and refused to do so on other days. She hated that he got a lump sum every month because he ran out of money in the middle and ate into her earnings.

'Go and stand in line with the rest of them every morning and carry the bag.'

'No,' he said. 'I am tired of running after cars, tired of bribing the caddie master, and bloody tired of fighting for tips.'

'Why? You think you are superior to the rest? Know your place. You are a daily wage earner. You have no pension.

I won't be around to take care of you when your liver says get lost.'

Old Man was the caddie for Big Man. Big Man was an addict who spent big money on golf. He bought a home in the hills in Kodaikanal next to the golf course. He travelled to exotic locations to scenic courses with his friends. He bought the latest clubs when they hit the market. And he engaged the best coaches to improve his game. Big Man was a poor player, a hacker, who moved heaven and mostly earth in his earnest attempts to be a good golfer. Large chunks of soil got thrown about when he played, and after he finished a round in Kodaikanal, it seemed the bison had invaded the course again and left their hoofmarks in the fairways.

He played thrice a week, alone if he had to. Single ball, it was called. A bird, a view of the setting sun, a tree in bloom, soft grass under his feet, a cross breeze, a dog at rest in a sand bunker, these were things that evoked feelings in him. Was nature the only reason he spent five hours sweating and burning up in the heat that Chennai produced every day?

'It is a game of half-truths,' he said when asked. 'I feel this is what brings people in and keeps them hooked.'

The whole truth, like a tournament prize, eluded him.

'You chase a small ball through hill and dale, rough and fairway, sand and grass, over water, under trees. You shape your shots, sometimes inadvertently.' He remembered fondly a high fade over branches onto a hidden flag. How could he forget that sudden low draw around a tree that hit the flag and went into the hole?

'You are called an amateur because that is an honourable status, not a comment on your ability,' said his uncle.

'The correct term for you is hacker.' His uncle was a good player, a scratch golfer in his heyday, and a stickler for rules.

Big Man was hurt. He joined a gym and worked on his core, hoping it would improve his game. The hacking continued.

'It is a mental game,' said his uncle.

Old golfers like his uncle were a pain. They were full of pithy statements and horny jokes. They were rule-bound, waiting to pounce on newcomers who hadn't memorised the Royal and Ancient's bible.

'We are a necessary curse,' said his uncle, 'because most newcomers are illiterate and uncouth.'

Big Man tolerated his uncle because the latter had helped in getting him a membership. He remembered standing in the bar waiting for his admission interview. He was wearing a suit. The trousers were tight because he sat on his arse longer than he should. He was nervous. He wasn't sure he had survived the test round. Despite having played the game for many months he could not play a round of 18 or under. His uncle had played with him on his test round and marked his card.

'Years of study have done me no good,' he told his uncle, after the round. 'I have studied the game. I have studied my swing. And I have learnt the rules.'

'And?'

'Truth is life sucks.'

His honesty struck a chord. There could be no other reason for his uncle giving him a leg-up in the committee meeting.

Yuva grew into his old man's sandals, became a full caddie, got a retainer from Big Man, and most evenings he drank himself into a stupor.

'The cheapest liquor is the best. I don't care how it is packed, what the bottle looks like, how it is poured and whether I am seated or standing. Usually, I am standing.'

It was a busy place, there were two-wheelers and cycles, people wearing helmets, the road smelling of piss. There was a concrete counter and booze was slapped down on it, money appearing from inside shorts which were inside veshtis, the notes grubby and wet. The shopkeeper was old and behaved like he was doing Yuva a favour.

'I am a regular and he does not recognise me.'

A half cut lemon turned its face, its two eyes were seeds. Salt was on the counter, a little wet, still good enough. Nearby was the sound of frying. Potatoes, banana fritters, aubergine slices, tomatoes. Red-brown coated, carrying the latest headline from the newspaper they were served in. Everybody was smoking. The labourers smoked unfiltered beedis, the office-goers smoked cigarettes.

'What happened to your father?' asked the shopkeeper, out of the blue.

'He died,' said Yuva, startled that the shopkeeper knew who he was all along.

Old Man had a large and forgiving liver that soaked the booze and his kidneys worked overtime and they chugged along for three decades till one small ulcer built up, gradually, into an abscess. The day it burst, the bleed could not be stemmed. Nobody was around to help him as his wife was woman enough to have dumped him. Old Man called Yuva, but by the time he arrived, his father had croaked. He left nothing behind by way of money or possessions. Whatever was of value was inside a safe in a pawnbroker's shop. Yuva went there looking to retrieve the stuff but was chased away.

Yuva was at his worst behaviour on the days Big Man did not play. Like his father, he refused to stand in line with the daily wage earners and carry the bag for someone else. The daily wage business was stressful. Some days you got stuck with badly behaved golfers who cursed the caddie for every mishap. Some days you were allotted the misers that most caddies avoided. Some days you rushed with the others to every car that came, and others got chosen. Each time you returned to the group, you either cursed or pretended to be crestfallen so others could laugh. Yuva and Mano, the ones with monthly retainers, would arrive just to watch. They would chat with the rest, crack some jokes and while away the morning.

Early afternoon was booze time. There would be standing space next to a six feet by six feet opening in the wall. A board hung by a nail and a couple of letters had erased themselves. What remained was ASMA BAR. T and C were missing from TASMAC.

'I should be going to college,' said Yuva. Both feet were on the ground, left knee was slightly bent.

'Me too,' said Mano.

Yuva was holding the bottle and it was half empty. Half of it was spoken for, the other half they would argue with through the day till it won them over.

'Bloody flirt this alcohol,' said Mano, slurring slightly.

'Cannot finish it before noon.'

'I know, I know.'

They had been warned. This was the road to early death, lined by livers, blood in their trousers when they peed, blood in their eyes when they woke up. Yuva kept the bottle in an inside pocket in his pants and his loose shirt hung past his hips.

'Nobody can see it.'

It had a simple shape and a screw cap. Yuva could open it with one hand. They drank it straight, from the bottle.

They liked to feel the spirit go down their throat, warm, on a good day some bite, and sometimes some taste.

'I don't like the taste. I don't know why they add it.'

'My piss smells. Sometimes my sweat smells. I don't know why they add smell.'

The days Big Man showed up, life was whole. Yuva would be sober, his hair combed. Like his father did before him, he would be philosophic, watching the hacking. Golf was a hard game, especially for those who lacked aptitude. There really was no one to blame after a while.

'Shoulder drop, Master,' said Yuva, when he couldn't take it any more.

Big Man broke a club occasionally.

'Chinese clubs, Master,' said Yuva, holding the splintered shaft. 'Cheap, but not good.'

Balls got lost in the rough ever so often.

'Committee making course difficult, Master,' said Yuva.

He did his bit, helping out, moving the ball ahead with his feet, improving the lie. Big Man became moody as he aged. Some days he shouted. Some days he was generous, uncontrollably happy when he made a long putt or hit his tee shot onto the green on a par three.

'His knees are giving him trouble,' said Yuva.

Mano shrugged. 'So?'

'I can see him struggle to bend and pick up the ball from the hole. Sometimes he struggles to bend and tee up the ball, but he insists on doing it himself.'

The weather was bloody in the summer, the sun naked like a flame. The heat rose from the ground, scorching the grass or what was left of it. The course was near the sea and there was salt in the air. Twelve months a year it was humid and muggy. At the end of a five-hour golf round, everybody was tired, thirsty and happy it was over.

'He is not my boss,' said Yuva. 'I can walk away.'

Mano laughed. 'Does he even notice you?'

'Sometimes we look at each other. He wants me to smile. He has never seen me laugh. He wants to. Sometimes he tips me heavily while looking at me.'

'And?'

'Thanks, Master, I say coolly. That's it. I take it and walk away.'

'Does he like you?'

'Yes. He tells me all kinds of private things. He was very fond of my father. He remembers him often.'

'He wasn't there at your father's cremation,' said Mano.

A crisis was around the corner. There was a dark golf round waiting to happen, a terrible day on the course when nothing would work, when the accumulated frustration of Big Man would turn on Yuva as the reason for it all. A change of caddie would be the last solution.

It was a tournament when the sordid deed happened. And Big Man was playing with his uncle in the four-ball and playing badly. After nine holes of watching the torture, his uncle spoke up. 'This game is not idiot-proof,' he said. 'There are fourteen ways to make a fool of yourself because there are fourteen clubs in your bag. On a bad day fourteen snakes.'

The smallest club had an open face and it was spiteful. It was called a sand wedge. Big Man had just fifteen feet to the flag and there was a sand bunker in between. All he had to do was accelerate through the stroke like Yuva had told him a million times. He stabbed at the ball and it plopped into the sand, cosied itself inside and only half was visible.

'Fried egg,' said his uncle, almost rubbing his hands, imagining what would come next.

The next shot flew low over the green and into the deep rough beyond. Yuva ran to find the ball. And then he turned away unable to look at what followed. Big

Man should have taken a penalty and a drop, but he did not because he had to show his uncle he could play his way out of the rough. He hacked the grass twice and the ball went in deeper each time. They couldn't see it now. Clumps of grass were strewn around, and some grass was on his hat and his clothes. Yuva looked away. 'Master?' he said.

Big Man took the sand wedge and hit a bench, once, twice. The wedge broke.

'I think you just killed a snake,' said his uncle.

At the bar, after things had cooled off, his uncle had some advice for his nephew. 'Change your caddie,' he said. 'Sometimes it helps. Don't ask me why.'

And so, it happened, just like that, for no reason at all. The abruptness was hateful, the lack of discernible reason hurt Yuva more than anything else. Yuva stayed home. Mano took his place on the course.

After a few days, Yuva joined the daily wage line, forcing himself to run up to the cars that came by. When Big Man's car showed up, he had to hide.

'Just do your job well and people will respect you,' his mother said. She said that to make him feel better, but he felt worse because he knew that as a day caddie he couldn't earn it. There were too many of them available, eager to bear with everything that the players threw at them, eager to cheat on their behalf. Respect was a rag that had been torn to bits, dragged by the foot into a daily wage hole that had them by the balls.

The next day he had no assignment. Yuva walked purposefully towards the practice range. The caddie master and part-time coach saw him approach.

'What are you doing here?'

Yuva ignored him. He picked up a bucket and walked a hundred yards towards the gaggle of young boys running around picking up balls. The boys saw him approach and began giggling. He stood amongst them, tall, out of place.

Fore, shouted one of the players. A ball described an arc, soaring towards the blue sky. Yuva needed no urging. He stumbled in his hurry and fell. He picked himself up and he ran.

This story won the first prize in Bridport Prize for Short Story in 2018.

The Magic Door

It was Sunday and Sampurna was on his knees in the washroom, his slipper in his hand. The drain cover in the corner had been set aside. He bent low over it.

'Why are you hiding?' he said. 'Come out into the open!'

Two tendrils emerged and flirted with Sampurna's nose. He sneezed. He slammed his slipper down but was late. The creature had disappeared. He rose with some difficulty and washed his hands. He considered using the spray can. It had a long nozzle that he could insert into the drain. He didn't have the heart.

He combed his sparse hair and set out for his morning walk. At the adda that he frequented, they discussed his reluctance.

'I cannot,' he said. 'I cannot inflict a slow death. The creature goes belly up and struggles when you spray it.'

'Dada, these creatures are invading your home.'

'I know,' he said. 'But that is no excuse for cruelty. They should put these spray manufacturers on trial.'

The adda burst into laughter.

'Dada,' said someone, 'the day you kill that roach, we will observe two minutes' silence.'

Sampurna Chatterjee was a playwright of note. He wrote political plays. In his spare time, he wished to bring down the government. The urge was strong and it interfered with his thinking. Any government would do. Central, state.

Even a local governing body. In the old days, all the proletariat needed was a riot.

'Times have changed, dada,' said his adda friends. 'These days you have to go online.'

The prospect frightened him. It was akin to coming out.

In the streets of Kolkata, a city he was in love with, the adda was the last outpost of the Resistance. His adda was near the Lake area, and most days after a bracing walk, he sauntered across to meet his group that gathered around a kerosene flame. The stove made a comforting sound and the tea was hot, served in small earthen cups. The group slurped, bandied epithets and vented opinions.

Sampurna's recent distraction was a young man called Ramu. Ramu had moved in as a paying guest with his neighbour Lodha. The Lodhas were Marwaris, a sharp business community that had a firm grip on commerce in Kolkata. Dada steered clear of Lodha but occasionally they met by accident. Their building was a four-storey structure on Sarat Bose Road and the apartments shared a small landing, a five square feet intimate space. Every chance meeting in the landing drove them further apart. A quick smile that bordered on a grimace, a rush to get past each other that resulted, more often than not, in an entanglement.

Ramu watched this ritual repeat itself. 'You cannot choose your neighbours, dada,' he said.

'Yes, I can,' said Sampurna. 'I don't recognise them as neighbours.' He pounded his walking stick on the landing. 'Who asked them to come to Bengal?'

He always had an unkind word for Marwaris.

'They think they are smarter than us. How is it possible?'

There were two festivals in the last quarter of the year that symbolised the divide between the two communities. The Bengalis worshipped the Goddess Durga, the symbol of Shakti, of feminine power and energy. During Durga

Puja, the city had a festive air with pandals sprouting in the middle of every street. Each pandal would have a Durga installation, priests would dance during invocations, and stalls would be set up offering books and homemade delicacies. Offices would declare a week-long holiday.

The Marwaris worshipped Lakshmi, the goddess of wealth. There was a festival a few days apart, in her honour, called Diwali. Every Diwali day, the prime devotee, Mr Lodha, had an oil bath, wore new clothes, lit incense sticks in his puja room, burnt camphor in a tablespoon and rang a bell. He also ate a vast quantity of sweetmeats and bought expensive gifts for his clients. Black Label whisky for income tax officers and the more expensive Blue Label for the commissioners. The street knew him for his speciality Diwali cracker, a long-lasting nuisance that was set off with fanfare in his presence. It was fifty feet long and time stood still when it got going.

Sampurna hated this muscular manifestation. The cracker created a smoke cloud that set him off on a coughing fit. He would emerge from it, tears in his eyes, shouting, 'You think a cracker can get rid of the demons in your account books?'

Ramu, like many others, celebrated both festivals. He tried not to take sides. This irritated Sampurna.

'You, from the south of the Vindhyas, declare your position.'

'Eh?'

Sampurna shook him by the shoulder. 'When was the last protest meeting you attended?'

'Never,' said Ramu. 'I am a South Indian, sir, a modest Tamil brahmin.'

'That you are. Mild-mannered, soft-spoken. A proper fence-sitter.'

'What is wrong with that?'

'Nothing wrong. By Bengali standards, you are hyphenated.'

They were standing in the small landing below a board that said Lodha and Lodha, Chartered Accountants.

'I worry about my future,' said Ramu.

'You should,' said Sampurna, 'but not too much. Even potted plants flourish these days.'

Ramu straightened the board. One day he would grow out of his current situation and have his own firm. Ramanathan and Company, Chartered Accountants. The thought did not enthuse him.

'I am at their mercy,' he said.

'There is one thing your landlords will do,' said Sampurna. 'They will instil the necessary shrewdness and selfishness in you.'

Ramu had to agree, being at the receiving end. He was an articled clerk with Lodha and Lodha. He was indentured labour, undergoing a four-year confinement in corporate record rooms. Audit firms were quiet places save for the rasp of pencil ticks, the click and shut of box files and the sound of stapling. Auditors wore thick spectacles and peered suspiciously at ledgers and supporting documents. They were paid to be suspicious, to be wary of clever company accountants.

Staying with his principals, the Lodhas, was a bad idea. Within their four walls, Ramu was domestic help. Once he had settled in, he realised he was busy running around fetching things and brewing tea for Mrs Lodha. In return, she fed him treats. Ramu discovered two things about her. She had her private stash of goodies that he had to ferry. And she had a private vocabulary, which he was privy to. Both were delicious. Some nights when her husband was asleep, she spent quality time seated at the dining table, indulging her senses. Ramu received orders and a tasting portion.

Ramu's late father had been a client of the Lodhas, and a close friend. Ramu's mother had entrusted him to them, sending him to work in faraway Kolkata because she had faith in Mr Lodha.

'He understands money,' she told her son. 'Your father used to say that in the Lodha household, money is a servant. Every rupee is made to sweat.'

Ramu's parents were as careful but money had their measure. They had very little to spare. Like many South Indians, they worshipped the Goddess Saraswati. She was the goddess of learning responsible perhaps for the army of engineers and software programmers who made their way into the USA every year. Saraswati took care of Ramu's grades but she couldn't help him plan his career.

Sampurna paid no heed to money and its temptations. This made him superior. The idea of worshipping a deity that represented wealth did not appeal to him. He was suspicious of people who did, people like the Lodhas.

'I have two questions,' said Sampurna, having bumped into Lodha on a day when his arthritis had acted up, robbing him of his walk.

'Yes?' said Lodha, unprepared and susceptible.

'Who is the master in your house?'

Lodha scratched his head. His wife was a qualified chartered accountant and to be fair she was more in demand with clients.

'What is your second question?'

'Why do you treat Ramu like your servant?'

Ramu, like most articled clerks, earned a pittance. There were better descriptions than an articled clerk in better vocations. Understudy. Apprentice. Trainee. Intern. Left to him, Ramu would have interned in a design firm. Instead, he was a foot soldier in an indentured army that went combing through a million vouchers. Vouchers were prepared by hand, attached to them were bills and receipts. The army drowned in them, ticked, tallied rows and totalled columns.

There were two exams that articled clerks had to clear: Inter and Final. Each had a single-digit pass percentage that was brandished by those who succeeded as a sign of natural selection. Ramu was in the middle of his tenure. Every morning he promised to turn this living hell on its head by kidnapping himself.

'An articled clerk has no narrative,' he complained.

'Indentured labour does not speak,' said Sampurna.

Ramu took a deep breath. 'I am going to change all this.'

'How? You are stuck in Kolkata, my boy.'

'Dada, one day I will stand in the Sunderbans,' said Ramu.

'And do what?'

'I will piss into the delta.'

He wept at the thought of submitting four of his best years to a stupid vocation, hunched over ledgers and reconciliation statements.

'I have forfeited my voice.'

He wanted to scream, say something colourful. He would surely go insane.

'Thank you,' he whispered, addressing his parents, 'for this misfit career.'

His hopes of a career in design were effectively dashed. Nothing new. The country was littered with smithereens, the remnants of shattered ambitions of young artists and troubadours. Ramu had filled in the application form of the

National Institute of Design in Ahmedabad. He remembered the showdown with his parents on the day of Sankranti. A day when kites soared, battles were fought, and some lucky ones cut themselves loose and drifted away, wandered into unknown fields and parks, and tasted freedom. He lost the battle that day.

'Tear it up. Now!'

He refused. He kept his unfulfilled hopes under lock and key and carried the form with him to Kolkata, just in case. Who knew what lay ahead? The city of Kolkata resonated with him. The Bengalis had their culture. If you pointed to them the poor state of their city, they pretended they were living a parallel existence.

Outside the window was a terrace. There were kites floating in the sky. The wind toyed with them. Boys in a nearby terrace tugged at sharp threads, chattering excitedly as their kites darted, dipped and soared. Children arrived in other terraces and soon it was an all-out war.

Sampurna leaned on his terrace wall and watched. Dark descended, the streetlights came on. On the street below, vendors were selling food items. Their children crawled on the pavement, chasing ants. Two women fought for place in the water queue, their curses sent the men into hiding.

The land where the roads of Rash Behari and Sarat Bose met saw the rise of vertical tenements, each four stories tall, each with four dwellings to a floor, an example of urban planning by the clerical cadre. This was state-decree housing. This was Bengali amnesia. The state forgot there was an aesthetic that needed to evolve beyond Satyajit Ray's cinema house and Rabindranath Tagore's Santiniketan.

There was no space to spare in his apartment. Rooms were small, the corridor that linked them was narrow. And Sampurna Chatterjee, Scrabble freak, a wingless infidel, a walking spellcheck and grammar doctor, stood in it and spelt subaltern.

Every morning he could be seen at the crossroads in his white pyjama and kurta holding his walking stick, shaking his head now and then, clearly unable to comprehend the plebeian architecture.

'This is culpable,' he said. 'My completed Scrabble board looks better than this.'

It was time to read Trotsky and fling his maid out. The woman came at 8 a.m. and dawdled till lunch, drinking cups of tea. In between, she chattered incessantly about her life. Sampurna had a heart but this assault was testing. It hurt him that his state was less than the sum of his brethren, each of whom was educated and culturally aware. His maid had a dulcet voice and could sing beautifully and yet all she did was harangue him, hoping to evoke sympathy or guilt.

She knew a smattering of English words. He decided he would teach her. Over a few months, he taught her a language that would help her break free from the prison of domestic serfdom. Once her grammar was in place, he expanded her vocabulary. They played Scrabble. For a week, there was silence. Ramu peeped in, worried and a little suspicious.

'She just got an eight-letter triple word score,' said Sampurna, beaming. Ramu came up and looked. She had spelt 'cheating'.

Sampurna began to notice a few things. His maid's blouse had tightened after the birth of her first child. Her breasts that were pert had now assumed a fullness that pressed against her blouse. Her blouse had hooks and a couple of loose threads. Her skin had a glow. She looked so well rounded. It seemed to him that all that had been reined in was now straining to break free. His game changed. He began to spell words like bodice and bosom, thigh and cheek, button and bed. One day he got 'bohemia', a land he had forgotten.

The maid left soon after to teach at a primary school. Sampurna was distraught at the sudden departure. But he bid her a fond farewell, even parting with a small bonus—a small tin of Lopchu tea.

'Don't boil it,' he advised her.

He placed a hand on her shoulder as she left, letting it linger. She met his eyes and held his gaze. She smiled. He remembered that smile.

The parting left an ache. Sampurna set out for a walk to clear his head. He spent the day walking on a common road, a proletarian pathway, a swath of rippled black with a tram track incised into it that stayed after the wagons were put away. One side of the road had commerce, the other had flags and protesters. People drove about on it as if someone had banned accidents. It was a curious time between Durga Puja and Diwali. Some pandals were being erected, others were being dismantled. That day the discourse at the adda was subdued. The group stood and sipped tea.

'You have used Sugar Free today?'

The shopkeeper nodded, a little anxious. His customers were temperamental.

'Dada, I believe your maid has left you?'

Sampurna grunted and said nothing.

'Who will you take up next, Professor Higgins?'

Ramu heard his name being called. For a change, it was Mr Lodha.

'Why is *he* calling you?'

'He is giving me accounting lessons,' said Ramu.

Mr Lodha had a set routine when he returned from work. It began in the living room with two servings of Johnnie Walker, half soda, half water, a bowl of salted cashew nuts, another with almonds, the business newspapers piled on a side table, the television tuned to a serial. After an hour of television and a cursory read of the papers, he would proceed to his throne at the dining table and wordlessly chomp his vegetables.

Mrs Lodha bore up with this, her manner betraying her frustration with evenings that had no purpose and were merely precursors to the nights. She yawned loudly and often. Ramu would stand near the kitchen door with a vacuous expression.

On weekends, Mr Lodha had the equanimity of a moth. He would sit for hours in a fixed place and nothing would ruffle him. Sundry visitors would arrive. Mostly they were people who listened.

At the appropriate time, Ramu would sit before Mr Lodha and open an annual report.

'Have you analysed the numbers?'

'Yes, sir,' said Ramu. His eyes had glazed after a while.

'The first time I saw a balance sheet I felt an emotional connect,' said Mr Lodha. 'It spoke to me. Every page had a story. And at the end, there were narrations that told me so much more. Did you read the director's report?'

'No, sir. You didn't ask me to.'

Mr Lodha clucked his tongue. A short, sharp lecture followed.

'The director's report tells you the story behind the numbers. In India, there are many variables. Power, water, manpower, pollution control, raw material, exchange rate, interest rate. These are variables. And what do they do?'

'Sir?'

'Each variable deducts a year from your life. You understand?'

'Yes, sir.'

'Imagine the voyage. Every month the conditions change. Every quarter the numbers add up, and if the results are rocky, the investors jump ship.'

After half an hour, Mr Lodha needed a break. He got up and left, shutting the bedroom door behind him. His wife, who was seated nearby, stirred.

'Young man,' she said, 'in the Lodha balance sheet you have only short-term value. You are what we call a current asset.'

Ramu smiled. 'And Mr Lodha is a fixed asset, madam?'

She mulled over that description. 'Yes,' she said. 'But fixed assets are subject to depreciation.'

Ramu ventured further. 'And our neighbour, Mr Chatterjee?'

She snorted. 'Sampurna? That loose cannon? He is a contingent liability.'

She left to join her husband in their bedroom.

An hour later, Ramu entered the kitchen, lit the gas stove and placed some water on the boil. The bedroom door opened, there was a flurry of movement, and Mrs Lodha entered the kitchen. Ramu was standing next to the fridge sipping from a glass of cold water. He was startled to see her. Her hair was loose and her clothes were in disarray.

She ignored him and set about making the tea. Ramu stood rooted, making no sound. She poured herself a cup and carried it to the dining room table.

'Come,' she said.

He followed her.

'Sit.'

He sat opposite her. There was a certain laxity to her posture. A looseness that Ramu had never seen. He dared not look closely at her. He could sense her ample assets were partially on display. She drank her tea with a slurp, drawing attention, letting her lips linger on the cup. He realised something and he was scared. He could look at her in a particular way if he wished to.

'He is not well sometimes,' she said, gesturing to the bedroom.

Ramu did not know what to say.

'There is some change since last year. The pegs are smaller, the drinking has slowed. Everything has slowed.'

She raised her hands and ran them through her luxuriant hair.

'He is getting heavier. His clothes have lost shape. He lacks patience.'

She looked at him. 'Some things need patience.'

Ramu held his breath.

'How old are you?'

'Twenty,' he said.

'What a lovely age.'

The cup of tea sat before him. He lifted the cup and his hand shook. She placed her hand on his and ran her fingers up his arm, her nails tingling his nerves.

'Speak to Sampurna,' she said. 'Ask that loose cannon about the magic door.'

Sampurna lit his third cigarette of the day. Ramu watched him inhale, saw a slight smile appear.

'Enjoying, dada?'

After the third puff, the worry lines on Sampurna's face disappeared.

'These fellows irritate me,' he said. He pointed to four young men sitting on a low wall. 'They are doing nothing in the middle of the day. What should I presume?'

'Unemployment?'

'I know where they stay,' said Sampurna. 'Their colony is a parra, a ghetto. They come here, sit all day and pass comments.'

He blew some smoke in their direction.

'When young people are not working and their arse is not getting kicked, there is a problem.'

'With the parents, dada?'

'No,' said Sampurna, stubbing out his cigarette. 'With the culture. With the civil society.'

'Heavy, dada,' said Ramu, adopting the local lingo. 'Heavy bhari.'

'What about those four grown men in the car?'

They looked at the old Ambassador vehicle, a taxi with many dents.

'Hundred per cent they are drinking and smoking. Four good reasons to repeal inheritance. Give it to the girls.'

'Girls smoke in Kolkata, dada. They drink too.'

'You want them to chant bhajans?'

Ramu threw up his hands. 'What is it you want to say?'

'In Ghariahat, it is raining. In Bhawanipur, there has been a sharp shower. Even the Alipore Police Station, that upmarket dump, has taken a drenching. Yet all I see is decay. No amount of rain can take away the accumulated decay.'

A few drops fell around them.

'It is obvious that my Bengal is dying.'

They sat for some more time in the light drizzle, waiting and watching.

'Something will surely happen,' said Sampurna.

Ramu fidgeted after a while. Was his elderly neighbour mocking him?

'My life is going nowhere, dada,' he blurted. 'I mean it is going in the wrong direction. You want me to sit beside you and wait for things to happen?'

'You think you are in control of your life?'

'I think so, I mean, at least partially.'

Sampurna lit another cigarette, cupping the flame. 'Couldn't you have lived it differently?'

'Of course,' said Ramu. 'How I wish I had!'

'Why didn't you? What were you waiting for? Divine intervention?'

'I wish I had met you earlier,' said Ramu.

Sampurna laughed. The rain was gathering strength and people dispersed in different directions. Ramu asked the question he had been meaning to ask.

'Dada, what is the magic door?'

Sampurna's eyes narrowed. He stood up and looked down at his young companion. 'Who told you about it? Did she? Tell me, did she?'

Ramu nodded. He assumed they were talking of the same person. 'She held my hand,' he said.

'Aha!'

Sampurna took a deep breath. What a woman! This Mrs Lodha was quite something. She was the Goddess Durga herself, asserting her presence in the house of Lakshmi. This Tamil boy was on the brink of something that could change his life. The poor fellow lacked the gumption.

A narrow lane called Broad Street had rows of open shops that abutted each other with thin partitions dividing them. The shops were crowded with material placed haphazardly on the floor. Partitions gave way often and inventory mingled only to be separated when a customer asked for something. Customers had to step around carefully. At times, they had to climb. The shops were dimly lit with naked bulbs that hissed when it rained, spat when they heated up and hurtfully died when wires shorted. The shopkeepers were a disdainful lot, untrained in the art of selling. They felt they did enough by merely plying their trade. They had to bid good money when sale notices came up in houses that were giving way to apartment blocks. Someone bought the girders, some the mortar, a few bought the bricks. The shopkeepers of Broad Street rescued the doors and windows. The doors were kept as is and were spruced up when a sale was made. Why bother polishing and painting if the weather lacked mercy?

Doors were stacked twenty deep with barely enough space to enter. These wooden seven by fours had witnessed lives, or so Ramu believed. The more interesting the door, the better was his imagination of what took place in the room. He scrolled through a row for a suitable door and a young chokra boy with hardened palms helped him. The owner was there but he wouldn't lend a hand. There was an interesting one, eight doors deep, and it needed strength to hold the rest at an angle so he could see the borders and the pattern. The shop owner wouldn't pitch in. On the contrary, his air of indifference persisted, unaffected by the grunts of the chokra. The boy strained his muscles while Ramu examined the door. A breeze blew into the shop, the owner's lungi fluttered. He spoke up.

'The wood for this door came from a jackfruit tree,' he said. 'It isn't the best wood to make doors.'

He said this with a shrug that implied—take it if you please, but remember I told you so. Ramu liked the door. It was like one he had seen in his grandfather's home.

'Why have you come here?' asked the shop owner. 'What is the real reason?'

Ramu realised he was a sharp fellow, a man with good instincts.

'I came looking for a magic door,' he said.

The owner stayed put, expressionless. It seemed he had not heard about that type of door.

'There is no magic door here,' he said. 'Don't waste my time.'

Ramu was undeterred. 'I need it,' he said. 'Sampurna Chatterjee sent me here. He said you would understand.'

On hearing Sampurna's name the shopkeeper changed. His air of indifference left him.

'Sit down,' he said, pulling a chair. 'Some tea?'

Ramu sat carefully. 'No thanks,' he said. 'I am in a hurry.'

The chokra received instructions. He disappeared into a row of doors, and after a while, he brought back a doorframe. An empty blue doorframe.

'All have not heard of this magic door,' said the owner. 'As you can see, it exists.'

'This?'

'Yes, this is the one.'

'What am I supposed to do?' asked Ramu. 'Take it home?'

'No. All you have to do is walk through it to the other side.'

Ramu laughed. 'Is this a joke?'

'No,' said the shop owner. 'Don't take it lightly. Remember, if you walk through this door there is no coming back.'

Ramu's feet led him to the blue frame. He paused and looked back at the shop owner.

The Writer

I stay in Whitefield, a suburb of Bangalore that has many malls, a lake and gated communities. The gated enclaves have Roman names. Their internal roads are called boulevards. They are paved with interlocking tiles and are lined on both sides with flower beds and decorative palms.

The entrance to the Il Palazzo enclave has free-standing pillars, the mansions have Corinthian columns and the clubhouse resembles the Parthenon. I dropped in on a Sunday to meet a friend and wandered around as I was early. I am a visual eavesdropper. It is what I do. Peeping into people's homes is possible in most Bangalore streets. Even a casual glance can lay bare a life being lived. Not at the Il Palazzo. Tall, trimmed hedges ring-fence each mansion. Brocade curtains hang heavy behind every window.

The place was quiet that Sunday. The wind picked up occasionally. Wind chimes whistled, small bells tinkled. Imported dogs picked up scents and poked their snouts through fences. A quick bark, a tail wag and they bounded away. I stood for a while, taken in by the orderliness of this little utopia. The clean lines, the cropped lawns, the paved driveways where the grass had been allowed to grow in small gaps along the edges, like liner notes in a symphony.

Staying in these affluent islands are expatriates and local millennials, their knobby knees hidden by Bermuda shorts. On weekends, they wear quarter socks and large sports shoes, speak in unfaithful accents and move around in terrible twos and threes. Friday and Saturday, they share their laughter over brews in pubs panelled with dark wood.

They watch football, eat sausages and cheer players who queue up at transfer windows and make millions.

I stay in a small house in a sixty-feet by forty-feet plot. I have an eight-year-old car powered by a three-cylinder 800cc engine. My wife works longer hours than I do. She has a regular job that takes her to an office ten kilometres away. I work out of home, spending most of my time in a corner that we call the study. It has one table, a laptop, space for A4 sheets and a pen stand.

I am used to days that have no set timings. I live and die by word count. I love days when what I have woken up with finds itself onto the page and survives. I am yet to publish a serious book. As a journalist, I write political columns, the kind that don't require travel or meeting people.

I hate people who question me about what I do. I hate questions about my income and who pays the bills.

What shattered this idyllic existence was suspicion of the worst kind, a self-fulfilling suspicion. I was sprawled on the sofa listening to the news. Someone had been killed. A writer in front of her house. Shot in the chest by a helmeted man who arrived on a bike. The incident was recorded by security cameras, which the police had duly seized. The unthinking constabulary released a still of her sprawled on the ground, some blood visible. She looked helpless and sad. I felt vulnerable. The image shook me and I had to change the channel. It took a while for my pulse to settle. I felt like calling somebody.

The slain writer had been targeted for her political views, her brazen stance, for her outspoken presence on social media. This wasn't the first instance of a writer being killed. It wasn't going to be the last. I had this suspicion, this sinking feeling, that I was next.

I did what came naturally to me. In that moment of stress, I sat at my table to write. And I wrote a scene in which someone walked up to me at my doorstep and shot me thrice.

I had started writing when I was young, and I had to face the silent scorn of a parent who could not fathom the indolence. For him, sitting in one place meant that life, in a sense, had ground to a halt. My father, a mild-mannered man, tried to persuade me to go out and lead an active life. He never had a minute to spare. His waking hours were spent on his feet. He had a job where he worked with his hands against the clock. He had a roster of friends whom he visited every other day. His friendships were quiet, and they endured in the absence of strong opinions.

My mother never shouted either. She was always around, a presence at the rear of the house, a place that she had made her own. She was a little hard of hearing, she read a lot, and it is fair to say she encouraged me in my journey with words. She was a librarian at a convent school nearby. At the time, the thesaurus and the encyclopedia were well-thumbed tomes. She was my hero. She stood up to my father and his subtle ways. They would meet me in the corridor that ran the length of the house.

'Don't you become a blue-collar like him,' she would tell me, in his presence.

My father would stand his ground but never fight. He had with him his quiet dignity that he polished to a fine degree.

'Playing chess with yourself again,' he said.

'At least he is using his brains,' said my mother.

'When will he go out and make some friends?'

I was writing. I was trying to write my way out of an ordinary existence. In a working-class household, it was quite something to move in and out of a narrative fashioned by imagination. Imagine the story. A life seeking a plot. The plot tethered to a killing.

Do you ever get this feeling, that you are seated with a large gathering in a cinema, looking up expectantly, and what unfolds on the screen is pretty much your life? I have this feeling, often. It is always dark, there is a hush, an anticipation, and then it begins. My life plays out in everyday detail. People get involved, nodding, laughing, clapping, whispering occasionally till there comes a moment when they are uncomfortably aware that what is unfolding before them is not going to end well. They cannot intervene. They want to but they cannot. They begin to speak to the actor on the screen. They shout and they holler, and finally the whole lot screams out at me in one voice.

I spent four years in a college, and it shaped my views. I was a student of literature and I was attracted to the writings of Nietzsche, Machiavelli and Marx. I preferred prose that was contemporary and of the moment—revelatory and incandescent. In my senior year, I was embroiled in the college election. I wrote lines for a rag, slogans for posters and small poems. I wasn't the public face of our faction. I liked what I was doing, lurking in the periphery and making a difference. The power of words in a political space. That was my lesson.

Politics changed in the years after college. Methods morphed. There were fewer rallies and more social media expression. Out of college, my political affiliations endured. A new party had use for the likes of me. I was cheap and available, a hot rod they could use to build a narrative, to stay relevant in a crowded online space. I had to come up with something every day, a clickbait or a deliberate provocation. In time, I built a handle that drew followers who looked forward to my slanted views on rampant capitalism, my curious twists on the headlines of the day. I was a kind of writer, putting words to use, their meaning taken to the limits of context.

My handle had no photograph. Nobody knew what I looked like.

I wrote about a crow. About my father. My old man. I never thought of him as old till he aged one day trying to get up from his cane chair.

The crows cawed outside our home. Everybody knows how the crow caws. Ka ka. That is also what we call it. A kaka cannot sing. Its caw lacks lilt, its tone has no texture. Through the year and its seasons, it sounds the same. The thing is the crow is aware of its limitations. It doesn't mean to sing.

The crow doesn't hide. It is not good-looking, and it has no disguise. There are better-looking birds like the koel, but the crow—it has intelligent eyes. They are curious. You can see the world through a crow's eyes.

In the heat, the crow simmers. By noon, it is a step away from exploding, its dark skin and feathers having absorbed the radiation. In the rain, it sits exposed, perched on a tree. It flaps its wings, shivers and caws. It doesn't complain.

My father is the same. Consider him a crow.

I came from an egg that the wily koel bird laid, as it does, in a crow's nest. It is all my mother's doing. I imagine my mother. I imagine her doing what she does best—surprising her child. She left us one day, taking my younger brother with her. She walked into the sunset, into the silver screen, and I looked up as she left, powerless, shouting. My grim-faced father sat next to me, holding me back. As tears dropped onto my shirt, self-pity struck a piano chord. In the distance, my mother turned one last time and waved.

My neighbour has a mango tree, a large one, and its branches have spread over my rear veranda. I like the shade and I do not mind clearing the leaves that fall. In season, the mangoes grow in front of my eyes and gradually ripen. A koel bird sings lustily as I sit with a cup of tea and survey the harvest. It is inevitable that I pluck a mango or two. My neighbour watches constantly. He can sense the temptation and is disturbed by it. He is older than me, a frugal man, bespectacled, and lonely, prone to counting the mangoes on my side. I fell out with him early on, when he introduced himself.

'I am an orthodox brahmin,' he said. 'You, sir?'

He was asking.

'I am against orthodoxy,' I said. 'I hold it in contempt.'

'I see,' he said, without rancour, blinking rapidly, weighing his response.

'Orthodoxy has its uses you know,' I said. 'It keeps a section of the population in rein. People like you.'

He looked surprised. 'I am a potential threat, sir? To whom?'

'To the idea of revolution,' I said.

'Are you an activist? Forgive me, I have never met one.'

He wouldn't go away. I looked towards the door and raised myself slowly.

'Is it worthwhile being a writer, sir?' he asked.

'Just look at what they are capable of. They killed old men, three writers. Why? Because they were rationalists. They were a threat to organised religion. Damn it, the biggest threat to religion is organisation. Then they killed a forthright woman for God's sake. What was she threatening? These people are casual and ruthless.'

My wife was dismissive. She thought nothing of my worries. She said my kind of paranoia was an idle mind's reaction. 'You are not that important,' was her reasoning. 'They will go after those who are well known, who have a national following, who represent something. You are just an online troll.'

I took no comfort from her summary dismissal. She was right in most matters but this time my instincts were strong. These guys were done with old-fashioned writers. They needed a writer who trolled. I was made to order, a member of a promising political party that had been formed in the last five years. Going against two national parties was a foolhardy enterprise. It was also a noble and heartfelt effort. Initial fumbles aside it was doing better every day.

'Something is going on in my vicinity,' I said.

'Vicinity?' she asked, raising an eyebrow. 'Or inside you?'

'I can feel it,' I said. 'You have to trust me. Writers have instincts you know. We keep writing crime till we can see it happen.'

'There is no plot, mister. No evidence that you are on any hit list. Are you being followed?'

'I am not sure,' I said. Should I tell her? She might laugh in my face. What could I say to make her take this seriously?

'Listen, I do not want to be found a crooked heap in front of my house.'

She shouted me down. 'Take your nasty suspicions for a walk. Don't come back till you have worked up some honest sweat. You will come back alive, trust me.'

'I have to stop writing before it is too late,' I said.

'Ha! You and your self-importance! What are you writing? It has a title?'

'Yes. Offence never rests. That is the title.'

In the scene that I was writing, I was scripting my own demise. I urge you to believe me. This is real, as real and unexplained as each of the previous killings. They are going to kill me in front of my house. Nobody will be there when it happens.

I stay in a locality that the municipality forgot. In this part of Bangalore, people need a place to throw their garbage. It has to be convenient and guilt-free. The popular spots are unused empty plots, stumps of fallen trees and a place that someone else has already used. I stay in a cul de sac with six houses on either side of a narrow road. Three cows roam the streets during the day and rest in our alley at night. At some mysterious hour, someone we have not seen milks them. He does not feed them and hence they roam the city foraging in the rubbish dumps. My house is the last in the cul de sac, on the left side. I feed two cats and a street dog, and they roam as they wish. I have a letter box that I have painted red, a birdbath that I fill every other day. There is a chikoo tree in front that fruits in season attracting young boys and girls from the neighbourhood. They pluck the fruit early, bite and waste it.

I write in the morning hours and then leave around noon for lunch in a nearby cafe that knows I will spend at least a couple of hours at a particular table that seats only one. I return for my afternoon snooze. I revise my writing till about six in the evening. I read for an hour and at seven I step out again for a drink. There are three bars nearby and

I choose by rotation. Anyone who has studied my daily life will realise I am a creature of habit. An assassin will pencil me in as a sitting duck.

I had this sense that I was being watched. I tried to shrug it off as silly paranoia but the feeling would not go away. I began to look around a lot more when I walked and when I sat in my usual spots. I was loath to change my routine. I tried to remember the faces I saw around me. The feeling of being watched is a creepy one. I became conscious. I stood before mirrors and looked at people behind me. I paused at street corners to see who went past. From my house, I peeped out of the windows.

The street dog began barking at odd hours in the evening. I came out when he barked and there would be nobody. The dog looked at a fixed spot across the street, his tail up, and he refused to move away. From the spot that he was looking at someone could take aim at my head or chest as I locked the gate behind me when I left for the bar. Whoever it was needed a small handgun. He could not miss from that range. I went to the spot where he would shoot from. There was space there for him to park his bike, a small tree beside which he could pretend to smoke, or answer a call, and then in a few short seconds take aim and shoot.

There were two cigarette butts. I took them away. Two days later, there were two more at the same place. The person was careless, he was an amateur.

The house harbours insects. It harbours their sounds. They strike up at odd times of the day and night. Every once in a while there is silence. I strain my ears, unused to the quiet, the quiet that occurs when every layer peels away. It can get queasy if this happens at night. I begin to imagine footsteps on the gravel outside, the low thrum of an approaching two-wheeler or somebody at the gate.

'Is somebody knocking?'

'Stop it,' says my wife. 'How many times will you make me get up? Why don't you go?'

'What day is it?'

A strange man dressed in white came to see me one evening. He rang the bell, walked in and surveyed my house. There were books everywhere he looked and that seemed to upset him.

'I know who you are,' he said. 'You are like the other mosquitoes.'

He asked me to quit the party and terminate my handles.

'You are inviting trouble,' he said. 'One day you will also get it.'

I should have been scared but I wasn't, not then. In a curious way, this man and his veiled threat gave some meaning to my existence.

'Why are you after writers?' I said. 'A writer is a pathetic person. Look at me, the state of my car, the age of my computer.' Pointing to the bookshelves, 'These,' I said, 'are the only things I value.'

He wasn't listening.

'I buy local rum from an army canteen, through a retired major,' I said. 'Because it is cheaper. I buy provisions from a bazaar that stocks material close to expiry.'

I wanted to tell him that I lived on very little, as did my parents. They were there on the mantelpiece looking at me, posing in a silver gelatin photograph, my father taller, my mother prettier.

He would not tell me his name, where he came from or who sent him.

'Think of me as a friendly warning,' he said.

I asked him to get lost. I chased him out of my house. Later as I sat down and thought about it, my hands went cold. Could this be happening? They knew where I lived. They knew who I was. This was them.

A slug is a piece of metal. Snub-nosed. It belongs to a chamfered tube into which it fits snugly. I can now say with complete certainty there is a slug that bears my name. It does not matter which gun fires it. That slug is mine. I know where it will enter, where it will exit. I am not very skilled at hiding but I wish to be. The knowledge of imminent demise is powerful, an elixir that works on my brain, the part that is programmed to resist death.

I examine my state of vulnerability and it is a joke. A pathetic one. If someone wanted to shoot me, they would be spoilt for choice. Remember the dead man walking, hearing the angels talking? My wound has begun to take shape. At the exact spot in my chest, hair is turning white. The skin is red and bruised. It is a site, a marked two-centimetre circle, waiting for history.

I thought of going to the police. I had never been to a police station, never met a cop before. Their portrayals did not inspire confidence. A visit to the police station brought some comic relief. I was laughing, not visibly, at myself. At my hapless state. Sitting in the station, I felt the situation was hopeless. I got to meet a senior cop who was terribly busy, occupied with inefficiency, prey to a poor method. He heard me out, and two sentences into my story, he held up a hand. Can you come back a little later, since it is not urgent? I tried to say something more; after all, it was a life-and-death situation.

There was an article in the newspaper the next day. It spoke of the gun. The gun had been used before. Its first target was an elderly male writer, a rationalist, a free thinker. He was shot in a domestic situation, by two young men who had studied his habits, his neighbourhood and chosen the time and place. They shot him outside his house in the evening when it was dark.

Then they shot the woman in Bangalore. There was footage of a young man wearing his helmet leaning over the compound wall, entering behind her and killing her. According to ballistics, it was the same gun.

Death ate into my being. I stopped listening to music. I found reading troublesome. I began looking into space, troubled thoughts bothering me. I died a little every day, every hour, every minute, in the small things I did not do.

I washed my face with soft soap, the water flowed into my ears and down my neck. I looked up at the mirror as I dried myself, cleared the glass of condensation. Outside, the city was settling into humid weather, dense clouds had camped at a few thousand feet and the wind had let off. It was still and quiet. I went up to the window and looked out. It was two-faced, Bangalore, like any other city. I could see the other looming, a presence, a what-if.

'Don't neglect yourself,' said my brother. He was younger, and wiser. He came when I asked him to. He could see the signs of carelessness. 'I don't like it. I cannot stand neglect.'

'How does it matter?' I said. 'How does anything matter?'

'Nobody is killing you in a hurry,' he said. 'Not when I am here.' He held my shoulders. 'I need to know everything. Any changes, even small ones. New people in the neighbourhood. Anybody following you.'

'I have nothing more to report,' I said. 'All I have are cigarette butts, a nasty feeling and uneasiness like I have never experienced before.'

We installed double locks and got the window screws welded. It took two days.

'Look,' said my brother, 'we don't know the enemy. One face, no name, no address. Only nationality and religion. And stupidity walking around with a used gun. What can we do? Think.'

'It has been killing me,' I said. 'Just thinking.'

'We could turn this place into a fortress and make you a prisoner. But that is worse than getting killed.'

'I could say sorry.'

'No, you will not. That is suicide. Don't be like that other fellow who started supporting the government all of a sudden. That is shameful. How will you live with that?'

'I could,' I said. 'People adapt.'

'Be serious,' he said. 'What can we do?'

'We should go to the police.'

'The police?' Like me, he looked doubtful. 'You think they will know?'

'I could go to the politicians,' I said. 'They are the ones who could find out. Or some senior bureaucrat. Do you know someone?'

We decided to make my home a fortress. We raised the height of the boundary wall. We installed a steel gate on rollers that was controlled by a remote. We installed cameras that covered the perimeter. Every inch was on tape, each tape was stored for a week and then erased.

We kept a dog, a mid-sized one. A cocker spaniel. A shaggy dog with black and white hair that we named Raavan. We chose him because his bark was really loud. Inside the house, his bark bounced off the walls. The sound was deafening and it made me feel better. Raavan was restless and could smell very well, hear things that I could not. It did not take much for him to get started.

Last of all, I wrote a piece, a violent piece, a denouement. I spoke directly to those who were waiting to take offence. Now it was just a matter of days.

We waited, my brother and I, unarmed, fear by our side, our only narcotic. I left home occasionally and returned before it was dark. Nothing happened.

'You have been proven wrong,' said my brother. 'Why are you sweating?

'I feel unwell,' I said. 'It doesn't matter. Death will find me sooner than sickness.'

'I sit on the cusp all day,' wrote the writer.

He strung new words together into sentences, framed his paragraphs carefully and collected pages from his printer. He read aloud from the page. His brother had left, and his wife had returned, as had a semblance of normalcy.

Every visit to the laptop yielded possibilities. Every day. The impossible was happening and he could not believe it. A book was taking shape. He listened to podcasts while he wrote.

'This language is so beautiful, so full of shadows. I have no idea what these words mean.'

'Urdu? Are you...?'

'Yes, I am watching Urdu Studio.'

'How many times will you watch that video?'

'Till I get the meaning.'

'I could translate it if you want me to,' said his wife. 'Should I?'

'No. That would take away from the experience.'

The koel bird that had taken residence in the neighbour's mango tree started to sing. A crow cawed.

'You should try and compose from what you have heard. Just use the words and you might come up with something.'

'Blind verse? No.'

Street vendors passed through the lane that day.

'Soppoaaeeya, soppoaaeeya,' shouted the regular vendor.

'Shall I buy greens today?'

'No, I have a tight feeling in my stomach.'

The vendor pushed his cart, his senses on high alert. Often a sale was because of his noticing passing interest. A curtain that fluttered, murmured conversation, a door that half-opened. When nothing stirred, he shouted.

'Keerai, keerai, keerai.'

'Say what you want, you cannot compose poetry,' said the writer's wife. 'Language is not the issue.'

'I don't agree. What is poetry? Simple things that need some adornment.'

'Hmmm. Could you switch on the water pump? The pressure is low. Please?'

He hauled himself up and walked slowly to the rear of the house where a small shed hid the pump. He bent low and reached for the switch. Two men arrived on a motorbike. The driver, wearing a helmet, alighted and walked up to the house gate. He peered over the wall. He saw his quarry walk towards him, eyes on the ground measuring his steps. The helmeted man looked back towards his companion on the bike and nodded.

They did it that day. They saw this man they had never met, never had a chance to speak to or get to know. In the name of an unknown master, a forlorn faith and a small sum of money, they shot him. Three shots rang out that morning. Caught the man in the chest. In close proximity, they burnt holes through him. The writer was shaken. He looked up briefly, a little bemused. It is happening, his eyes said. I told you, he mumbled as he fell. His wife wasn't listening.

THE SCARECROW

It was spring, the first seeds were planted. Green shoots appeared, then summer rain. Months later, a plentiful crop. He stood in a thatched granary bursting at the seams. Something woke him up. He lifted his head; he heard his neighbour shout.

'Dai Dorai! Your bulls need feeding.'

At the farm, the mornings were busy, no respite. His wife fed the cows, they gave plentiful milk; the bulls for some reason had to be fed by him. He washed his face, mumbled a prayer and headed to the field. The land needed tending, it needed water.

On the whole, the weather was kind. In the plains of Tamil Nadu, the sun did its job, the clear sky was its accomplice. Rain troubled the farmers, it was whimsical. They prayed, the village panchayat conducted pujas, the women walked miles to the open well. The village was a small one, Chinnapuram. Croppers who stood in the middle of their plots could see the bunds that marked the edges.

His neighbour, the one with the loud mouth, was a dung beetle, a drinking companion who broke into lewd songs. He was a nuisance at night. In the village quadrangle, he had weaponised the public piss.

There were landless labourers in the village, Dorai couldn't afford them. He worried as he aged, his body bent, muscles withered. He was an old-fashioned farmer who ploughed his holding with his two bulls. He had trained them with his whip, they made orderly furrows. He had to crouch to plant seedlings. Snakes blew bubbles and swam away. In a small patch, he threw seeds in even patterns. He was thrifty with water like most farmers in Tamil Nadu.

Dorai was good-looking—when he was young. Wind whistled when he spoke through gaps in his teeth. Dirt accumulated where his nails had chipped. His skin was well-worn with cuts near the grain. Past middle age, he was a map of the land he inhabited, a visible way of life that cut close to the bone. He tried to comb his scraggly hair and broke two combs. He threw his head back and laughed.

He had faith in Ayyappan, the all-powerful son of Shiva and Mohini. His Ayyappan was a framed portrait at the base of a tree that had a convenient hollow. Every morning Dorai bent low, touched the ground with his forehead and lit an incense stick. He murmured what sounded like a prayer, words merged into musical notation.

'I won't die, you will grow up. Then?'

Dorai's son Rajesh was a rascal. 'I don't think about these things,' said Rajesh. 'I am not like you.'

'This land will not support two families.'

'You are to blame,' said Rajesh. 'You stay here, I will leave.'

Youngsters were fleeing to the city. There were rumours of better prospects, stories of sons and daughters who sent money orders to their parents. Dorai's son had no plan. He had three friends, the group was called a kootam, each was called a kootali. They prided themselves in being rough. Raju was a stylist; he wore a coloured kerchief around his neck. Mani had bravado; he was a banda type. The third was plain violent. The four were happy in their communal upbringing. They fought for small things with intensity. They fought for fishing rights in the deep end of the pond.

On festival days, they fought to be the first to pull the thick ropes of the temple chariot. They played games that had a violent streak.

Kite flying with its glass-fed manja cuts.

Bambaram or top-spinning with its nail-gouging marks called okkers.

Gilli danda with a hefty stick that, with a 'thak tip tip thwack', sent a sharpened projectile on its way.

They fought till the light faded, till they could hear the flutter of bats and the rustling of snakes.

It was a daily spectacle.

'What will they grow up into?' asked Dorai.

The other village elders snorted. 'English-speaking showpieces,' said one.

'Alagurajas, behaving like royalty in their bush shirt and full pant,' said another.

'Aalinals, and master of none,' said his neighbour.

'You old people are to blame,' said Rajesh. 'You taught us useless things.'

'Loosu fellow. You think you are smarter than us?'

'I will be,' said Rajesh.

He got into trouble. There was a girl that the other boys chased. The youngsters were reckless, they chased her and she ran, and when cornered, she jumped into the large pond. Rajesh was around and he stood up to them. He was beaten up. That night, the boys were sleeping, they awoke screaming, ants crawling over them, some rats nibbling their toes. Somebody had poured honey on them and their clothes. Rajesh hid in an abandoned hut but they got to him. This time he was ready, he had a scythe.

'You better leave,' his father said.

His mother Rukmani fainted when she saw the blood.

'Not mine,' he said.

'Go,' said his father. 'Leave!'

He went, first to a town that had an uncle and an English-medium school. He spent time in the local cinema, in tea stalls, in the company of others like him. He was above average height, swarthy, good enough for a reputation. He passed school exams using chits. He gained admission to Pachaiyappas College in Chennai in an obscure course. Pachaiyappas was famous, an institution favoured by roughnecks readying for a career in politics or policing. Students bored with studies went on strike. They burnt a bus, they threw some stones and, to round things off, they went to nearby Loyola College and chased some wimps. Things changed when he met Gowri.

Gowri, an honours student in Stella Maris College, was meant for better things. Rajesh would be her one big mistake. She just liked him a lot, she knew what he was about. They met in coffee shops, she rode pillion on his bike, they saw films, they visited the beach. She quarrelled with herself and yet succumbed.

'People call you a rowdy, Rajesh.'

What could he tell her?

'Are you a troublemaker? That's what people are saying.'

'I am a student leader,' he said. It was a fertile ground for a career in politics.

Gowri came from a middle-class background. She liked the hint of madness that Rajesh had, an uncontrolled element that she found attractive. He wasn't predictable, vacillating between the tender and the profane.

'I have a job offer,' said Rajesh.

'From?'

An unknown organisation. The job had no description, there were no fixed hours and payment was in cash.

'They like me,' said Rajesh. 'The pay is good.'

She believed in herself, ignored his promises and her foster uncle's warnings, and they set up home. A few months later, they formalised the arrangement. Rajesh informed his parents, his mother showed up and got along famously with Gowri.

'Please visit your father,' Rukmani said before she left.

Rajesh was busy. It wasn't a regular job. He was busy in the evening, sometimes at night. He got things done, when asked he chose not to elaborate. Gowri was pregnant. When the rains started, she pushed him to visit the village.

After a couple of days in the village, he began complaining.

'Nothing changes here,' he said.

The two trees were there, the temple, the local elders, the two kootalis, each a little older with chips on their shoulders and axes to bear. Rajesh began to flail. He fought with his father.

'Why do you behave like this? You look like you want to run away.'

'I will.'

'You look angry. Who are you angry with?'

Rajesh was frustrated his father never changed. He was in a mould that had formed around him.

'Why does he stick to doing the same thing?'

'Out of necessity, kanna,' said Rukmani.

'Why doesn't he try new techniques, new crops?'

'He has constraints, raja.'

'It is so frustrating!'

His mother spoke softly. 'It is a form of helplessness,' she said. Rukmani had kind eyes and kind words.

'I cannot stand around and watch.'

How he wished his mother had more of a say. All she did was what she was told. That was her training. She never complained. During the day, she was busy milking cows, managing the house, the dung, the feed, the pots and pans, the endless clothes. In later years when she visited her son's family in the city, they kept her busy. She seemed happy, they never asked. Dorai never provoked her, he was afraid one day she would say something. That day never came, and when she died, father and son were left wondering what she would have said, what had she really felt?

Rajesh remembered a night when he was six, he awoke, a song was playing loudly on the radio. Bleary-eyed, he peeped into the main room, he saw his mother dancing. She was alone, her saree tucked between her knees, moving with felicity and abandon. The song playing was 'Rukkumaniye, para para para'. It was a playful song with modern moves.

'Amma,' he said, surprised. She stopped midway through a twist. 'Kanna?' She picked him up in her arms and danced till the song ran out.

'You are dancing?' he said.

She laughed, set him down and loosened her saree, stood before a mirror and adjusted her blouse.

'Once a year, on one night,' she said, 'the brahma kamalam blooms.'

It was true, the brahma kamalam flower made a rare appearance. People stayed awake nights to watch it bloom.

Panic gripped Dorai when Rukmani passed away. He was rudderless, single, unable to confront his situation. Dorai sought help from neighbours. He wrote to his son, a long, rambling letter full of mistakes that promised self-harm and ended abruptly. He stood in the field all day, a stout stick across his shoulders, his arms spread over them. Birds flew by, none alighted. He looked forlorn, exposed to the elements, a scarecrow.

In the city, Rajesh was busy, he had a new energy. 'I have ideas,' he said.

'Good ideas take root in unlikely places,' said Gowri.

'What?'

Gowri was working on him. Under her tutelage, he read books to improve his English. He read self-help books that promised to unleash his inner Ferrari. He wished he was smarter, that he could move away from the physical nature of his current job.

Gowri continued to challenge him. How far would her husband rise, was her question. She was on the verge of doing something herself when they had their first child. She had analytical skills and a feel for numbers. She solved puzzles with ease, she decimated the daily crossword. Watching over milk made her blood boil. Twiddling her thumbs is what she called raising her children. Domestic life in her case would lead to violence.

The old man was unhappy. His son's apartment in Chennai had three bedrooms, his wasn't the smallest but it had no toilet. He shared one with his two grandchildren. It had a western commode. He was used to crouching, Indian style.

'What is the problem with western?' Rajesh asked.

Dorai screwed up his face. 'No pressure,' he said.

This was his first visit to the city. His village was just four hours by bus. He missed it. Seven days in the city and he felt like a migrant. He had surprised his son by showing up. Rajesh had barely mentioned a visit.

It so happened it was a bad year in the village. A poor harvest followed by water scarcity. It was the month after his wife Rukmani had passed. Without her, the days felt long and the homestead was in disarray. The animals were restless, reproachful when they looked at him. He spoke to his neighbour, there was no key to hand over. He packed some belongings and fled.

When he arrived in the city, the hate was instant. It was 11 a.m. and he was pushed out of the bus. He collected his dented suitcase. The sun was out in strength. For some reason, his sandals felt heavy. He realised the road tar was wet. He caught a crowded local bus. People stared at his white dhoti that was tucked between his legs, his long, droopy moustache and the old-fashioned money belt around his waist. His suitcase knocked people's knees and crushed somebody's toes.

'Vadhyare,' shouted someone, 'this is a city bus, not mofussil.'

'Vadhyar is running away with his suitcase,' said another. 'Going for a kacheri, thatha?'

He got to a window seat. He wiped his forehead, looked out and was awed by tall cranes that were weaving a giant web. Closer to his son's place, there were buildings with balconies where undergarments were drying. He walked from the bus stop. Vendors with food carts guided him to Rainbow Colony. He smelt the old oil they were using; he saw the dirty bucket of water that was used to clean plates.

The apartment was empty when he reached, the key was below the doormat. He followed instructions and had lunch. Then with nothing to do, and feeling hemmed-in, he let himself out. He spent a couple of hours under a tree. Across the road was a school, nearby a hospital with an Emergency Room. He stood still and watched, heard the loud voices and sirens, and imagined what went on in the lives of people he would never meet.

His bladder was full. He used a public toilet. They charged him a rupee.

Rainbow Colony was a dense development. Dorai found the concrete overbearing. He felt cramped. Cars were parked bumper to bumper, some bikes squeezed in between. The garbage bins overflowed. Plastic packets flew into trees, used sanitary pads spilled out, and street dogs smelt blood and tore them apart.

'Sariyana assault,' he said.

There was constant bickering between neighbours. From time to time, the electricity transformer sparked and flamed. In the night, the community cats mewled.

His son went to work, the grandchildren to school. There was his daughter-in-law Gowri and him in the apartment. She had thin lips and restless eyes. She saw everything, her eyes followed him. He couldn't stay inside, with her there. She did not resent him, she said so to his face.

'I used to work,' she said. 'I stopped because of the children.'

The two boys were a handful.

His wife Rukmani used to come twice a year to help out, and she was welcomed. They wouldn't let her go back. Three months would elapse each time. Dorai did not accompany her on those visits, he wasn't invited.

'Please understand,' Rukmani had said, 'nobody there has time. Who will look after you?'

'Do you play chess?' asked Gowri.

'No.'

'Scrabble?'

He shook his head.

'What shall we discuss? Shall we discuss something?'

He asked for a Tamil newspaper, and halfway through the front page, he fell asleep. Gowri threw up her hands. She locked herself in her room and played loud music.

He woke up, wore his sandals, a slight scowl, and he left. There was a park nearby, open through the day. It had a large lawn encircled by hedges, a walking track and a fence. There were stone benches below trees. He spent hours there by himself. He looked balefully at what was bothering him—a tap that was dripping. On the way home, he stepped on a rubbish heap and a foraging dog almost bit him.

Cooking smells greeted him as he entered the building. His stomach churned. He yearned for traditional food and rustic ingredients. He was sick of cottage cheese cubes, white rice and brown bread. He was sick of the ladies' group that assembled at home. They were noisy and condescending. He preferred the company of standing crops, birds that slept during the day, night owls that stared without malice.

When he held his coffee mug, he wondered who made it. Its perfection hurt him, more than its shape.

The rains started. For a day or two, he did not step out. He got into a fight with Gowri and words were exchanged. When Rajesh returned in the evening, Gowri complained. She told him her side of the story. He got an earful from his son. His two grandchildren stood and watched.

The next day, it rained again. He stepped out with an umbrella and sat in the deserted park. Raindrops splotched on the tar road and clattered on tin sheets. Water flowed, collected the refuse on the roads and formed lakes near the drains. He returned to the apartment after a couple of hours, happy and wet.

'Enjoyed?' asked Gowri.

'Went for some air,' he said in Tamil, 'came back with a poem.' It was the first line of a song he loved.

His son shared some rum that evening.

'Rain is different in the village,' said the old man. There, rain fell on leaves, on thatch and on domestic animals that flicked their tails and shivered. Rain formed streams that fed a small lake held together by a bund.

'Appa,' said Rajesh. 'Are you happy here?'

He looked away and shrugged. 'Was Rukmani busy when she came here?'

'She used to play with her grandchildren. And she cooked a lot.'

Rukmani's cooking had a particular taste that came from first principles. Fresh ground masalas, honest ingredients and a slow fire.

'Do you miss her?' asked Rajesh. 'Sorry, silly question.'

His son had no idea how much he missed his wife. He felt alone, so alone that he had come to the city, braved it all, standing in its midst like a sore thumb. Despite everything, he felt better in the city in his son's house. He couldn't bear the thought of returning to the village.

'Appa,' said his son, 'you look sad and unhappy sitting alone in the park every day. The neighbours think we have been fighting.'

'Should I…'

'No, no, stay for as long as you want. Whatever makes you happy.'

Nobody questioned his habits in his village. In the city park, the gardener leaned on a spade and confronted him. 'Are you waiting for someone?'

'Should I?'

'What were you doing in the village? Sitting like this?'

'Not sitting, standing,' said the old man. 'I was the village scarecrow.'

A young couple, doctors from the look of it, noticed him. They observed him closely. They came up to him.

'Could you tell us your name?'

He twirled his moustache. 'No,' he said.

'Do you have your address, Uncle?'

'Yes,' he said.

'Should we take you there?'

Rajesh laughed when he told him. 'They probably thought you were suffering from something.'

'Alzheimer's,' said Gowri, 'or dementia.'

It was the city that was wacko. People were clearly out of sorts, in a permanent hurry. Their daily routine was mental. Dorai sat quietly in his park amidst the hullabaloo. He went twice. He sat in the evening as well.

Chetan, a man with a limp, appeared as he did every day. That day, instead of limping around the park, he came up and confronted Dorai.

'Dirty old man,' he shouted. 'Sitting there and eyeing the women.'

'Moonji paaru,' said Dorai in Tamil.

'What?'

'You think I am sitting here sighting these mamis? These old kelavis? Why do they wear such tight clothes and walk?'

'What the hell?'

The next day Chetan brought his dog, a big Alsatian that strained on its leash baring its teeth.

'Look at my dog,' he said. 'See, he doesn't like you. Don't come here again.'

Despite this, the old man was there the next day. Chetan appeared but walked past the park. The old man got up and followed him. They walked slowly to the bus stop. It wasn't rush hour; the bus would be empty. A few minutes later, it arrived, its brakes made a metallic sound. They boarded the bus. He sat at the rear; Chetan walked ahead to the front.

A few stops later, Chetan rose. He seemed unsteady. He held on to the seat rail, then the suspended handgrips and stumbled to the exit as the bus slowed down. He almost fell onto the road. As the bus left, he crossed the road. He did not see the truck that came from the opposite side. The sound was a sickening thwack, Chetan flew. His head hit the road and that was that.

The old man rushed home. Was this really happening? It felt like a dream. When his son returned from work, he told him the whole story.

'I am feeling feverish.'

Rajesh felt his forehead.

The next day, his father brought the newspaper report.

'See, I wasn't dreaming. This saavugraki, bloody suicide type, was threatening me. Look what happened to him.'

Rajesh didn't know what to say.

'What were you doing on the bus?'

His father shook his head in wonder. 'I have no idea.'

'Do you know where that bus goes?'

'No, Rajesh.'

Gowri was fed up with the situation. Her father-in-law showed no signs of leaving and her husband refused to discuss the issue. She tried every trick. For breakfast, she threw some cereal in a bowl, added milk and set it in front of her father-in-law. The old man stared at the bowl. It looked like dog food. For lunch, she gave him a bowl of soup. It was thin gruel, light brown in colour and some pieces of vegetable floated in it. The old man wasn't sure what he hated more, the soup, the plastic bowl or Gowri's sullen attitude. Dinner was a small mountain of under-boiled rice.

The old man said nothing. He ate what was given to him without complaint. He knew what was going on. From time to time, he looked at Gowri and smiled.

'Why are you smiling at me?' she asked.

'I was remembering what Rukmani told me about you,' he said. 'She said don't be fooled, that little one is handling your rascal son, she has to be clever.'

He squeezed himself into the tiny balcony and lit a country beedi. He placed a clove into his mouth to deaden his sensitive teeth.

He had trouble with the building lift. It was a noisy lift with a loud recorded voice that kept saying, 'Please shut the door, please shut the door…' The lift had a black sliding grill and a wooden door. Getting in, he had to open the door, hold it, slide the grill to a side, get in, slide the grill back fully and wait for the door to shut. All this took a while and he had to listen to 'Please shut the door'. This made him nervous. Invariably his hands would get caught in the grill. Once, he changed his mind, threw out his hand to stop the door and almost lost his fingers.

He saw Gowri, she was standing outside the lift watching him struggle. She was laughing.

He began using the stairs but couldn't handle the climb. He decided to master the lift. He went up and down in it for half an hour, causing a major commotion. People came out of their apartments to check. The building secretary came up to him and spoke harshly. He called him names.

The old man called him one in return, just one. 'Saavugraki,' he said.

'What did you say?'

'Morattu payale,' he said, for good measure. Proper suicide case.

Rajesh was informed and he had to apologise.

'Why did you curse him, Appa? What is this new habit?'

'Just for thamaash,' said the old man.

Two days later, the building secretary stepped out in the morning to buy vegetables. Dorai for some reason went along. He had never been to the market before and he wasn't planning on buying anything. He just went along. The secretary bought a bagful. He walked slowly, holding the bag, leaning to one side. Dorai was a few feet away when a speeding motorcycle hit the secretary and broke his leg. The next day, they brought him home in an ambulance. Dorai and Rajesh were waiting for the lift when they wheeled him. They let him go first. When the lift went up, the old man smiled.

'Appa, why is this funny?' asked Rajesh.

'I saw it happen,' he told his son.

'What?'

He told him how it happened.

'But why did you go to the market?'

His father had no idea. He couldn't forget what happened. He kept smiling.

That night, the old man climbed to the terrace and smoked a beedi. Rajesh came up.

'Are you bored, Appa?'

'Not at all.'

'You are happy?'

'I haven't come here to do anything.'

'I see.' Rajesh was at a loss. 'Is everything fine in the village?'

'I am afraid of going back,' said his father. 'When your mother died, the sky had dark clouds, there was a storm in the village, and as I stood in the field like I usually did, I thought I would be struck by lightning. I ran, I fell, but still I ran. In the kitchen, pots and pans started falling. I went out and tried to milk the cows and they kept kicking me. By then, the dogs were barking, the hens scattered as if there was a jackal between them. I was convinced Rukmani had come back as a ghost. The night after we cremated her, she came to me in my dreams. She couldn't stop talking.' The old man stubbed his beedi. 'I lost my senses. I wanted to harm myself, but I couldn't. That's why when you said, come, I came running.'

Rajesh was worried. He asked an office boy to keep a watch on his father. The boy sent in his report.

'Your father sat in the park in the same spot. Three hours morning, three in the evening. Nothing happened for two days. No one came up to him. He smokes a lot, drops the beedis on the ground, grinds them with his sandal and leaves them there. Today, someone objected and they got into an argument. The passer-by shouted at your father, he sat there and ignored him. That irritated the man. He began to get physical. Your father looked at him and suddenly he smiled. Dai saavugraki, he said, if you touch me, something will happen to you. The passer-by caught hold of your father's collar. What will happen, he shouted. I had to intervene. I calmed the passer-by. I have his number if you want to speak to him.'

Rajesh was horrified, not by what had happened but by what could happen. He called the stranger and apologised.

'He has come from the village,' he said, by way of explanation.

'You think I don't know what saavugraki means? Do I look like I want to die?'

'He is a simple person,' said Rajesh. 'Don't take him literally.'

The passer-by relented.

'And by the way, please be careful.'

The man was confused. 'Sorry?'

'Just a friendly warning,' said Rajesh, making matters worse.

'Are you threatening me?' shouted the passer-by. 'What do you mean, be careful?'

The man called again after a day. 'I know who you are,' he shouted. 'Mr Rajesh, you are a thug. Everyone knows.'

On the weekend, the old man was seated in the park when Rajesh approached him. He made space on the bench. They sat together for a while.

'You don't have to do this,' said father to son.

'I am worried about something,' said the young man.

'What?'

'I heard Gowri hasn't been treating you well. Is she bothering you?'

'Doesn't matter,' said the old man. 'These are small things.'

'It does,' said Rajesh. 'If she isn't, don't worry, I will speak to her.'

'Okay,' said the old man. He got up from the bench.

Rajesh was looking at him. 'Why are you smiling?' he asked.

Forbidden

We are surrounded by space. We cannot get away from the emptiness. There are acres and acres of fallow land with low brush, rocks and drones. The drones are everywhere, buzzing like flies. We can see them from a window; low down we can hear them. We are allowed one window. The rest have been boarded up, by order. More than one window causes depression.

Some days when I go out, there are shouts of 'Get back inside!'

When the first bombs went off, we did not hear them. They happened far away. The wind carried the destruction. It took away the leaves, leached the soil and singed our eyebrows. The blinding light left a white layer on the topsoil that looked like salt.

We were asked to stay away from cultivation.

Our houses are made of reused material and they stand on stilts. They struggle to stay erect. When the wind howls, they sway and most times they return to even keel. Mine listed to a side and stayed. I felt the slant in my knees. When I lay on my bed, the large dresser loomed, the floor creaked when the weight shifted. The stilts are for an imaginary situation. Somebody predicted a great flood. We were not taking chances. Not after the fire that came from the sky.

A month passed by without electricity.

Thirty days I hadn't seen the corners of my room. 'There is no more coal,' someone said. 'And the reservoirs are empty.' I learned how to use flintstones. For fun.

'We are going back to a golden age,' said the Mayor, at our Town Hall meeting. 'Pre-carbon. Post-atom.'

I stared at what was on my plate, at the morsel on my fork; a strange taste hovered on my tongue.

'What is this?'

'Cordon bleu cooking,' said my mother.

'It tastes like shit.'

'I thought you had no time to be rude?'

'I am not being rude. This is not what food is meant to be.'

'Darling,' she said, 'I started with an original recipe. The key ingredients are not available any more. I did what I could.'

I couldn't believe that was all we had to eat. There was no getting away from what was on my plate.

'It tastes like shit. It looks like shit.'

She made some kind of sound. 'We look like shit,' she mumbled.

'Could you look at me while you are speaking?'

She looked up. 'I am typing, as you can see.' She typed with one finger on her old typewriter and peered at every word.

'Fine,' I said. 'You eat this. I cannot. I will leave you in peace. You can sit here and dream of the star of Michelin. One day it will shine over you.'

My mother wrote cookbooks. She was a successful author with a following. She had a way with words and she could tell a story. She was not, by any stretch of the imagination, a good cook. And that upset me. Her books were printed by hand in small batches and there was a queue at her readings. Each recipe of hers was a story that, in the absence of ingredients, sent the imagination soaring.

'What lies are you writing today?'

She screamed at me. 'Why don't you go out and get me something,' she shouted.

'What?'

'Forbidden,' she said. 'If you know what that means. And clean up the oven.'

I left for the bar. On the way, I walked past the hill. There were four houses on the hill that you could see from a distance. They were painted in bright colours and they had chimneys. Nobody stayed in them, in fact, nobody walked the road up the hill. It seemed the hill was on bad land waiting for somebody. Deep cracks had formed, spreading out from the epicentre that lay beneath. The hill looked ominous, vaguely threatening, a bit like a spider waiting in its web.

The bar served alcohol that tasted like spirit. The colour was clear water. I drank two shots quickly and waited for half an hour for my mood to improve. The place was open for just two hours. It ran out of liquor every day. There was a woman my age in the room. She came in like I did, sat alone and drank water. She looked at me and I made an involuntary gesture. She knocked on the counter, the barman came up to her and they spoke. The barman looked towards me, smiled, and said something to her. She walked up to me.

'Shall we step outside?' I said.

'I do not smoke,' she said.

'Come for the weather then, come for the sky.'

Outside the bar was a small quadrangle encased by brick walls. It was dark and dank. We stood, leaning, and looked up to check on the stars. The smog clouds of war had voided the sky.

'Nothingness,' she said. 'I like nothingness.'

I left home the next day looking for barter. I would offer my labour for a basket of ingredients. I would surprise my mother and help her bring a recipe to life.

The most prosperous citizen in our settlement wasn't a tradesman. He was a painter of signs. 'To-Let' was selling well, he said. As was 'Everything Must Go'. He saw my list and ticked a couple. He told me where to go next. I headed towards a second-hand car dealer.

It was late morning. Dew lasted till noon. The sun struggled because the sky had a lens, a grey shade of Aviator Ray-Ban. The first to feel the lack were the leaves. Then skin, then moss. Enormous mushrooms grew, the size of a bush. Eczemas thrived, forming continents.

'Rain will wash the sky one day,' mother said. 'The sun will get back its strength.'

'There will be tulips soon and sunflowers,' I said.

She smiled. 'In my dreams, every pond is full of pink lilies.'

I reached the second-hand dealer's yard. He was busy removing seats from the vehicles. There was a large mountain of car seats in a corner.

'How come you are making money,' I said. 'There are no cars on the road, nobody is driving them.'

'More and more women are buying,' he said. 'They want big cars.'

His yard was on the grounds of an abandoned church. The disused plot had weeds and a chipped building with gargoyles and a gnarled steeple. Our Lady of Arthritis, we called it.

'Say again?'

'They are living in the cars,' he said. 'I remove the seats and it becomes a room. If you look into the bonnet there are no engines. They use that space for storage.'

He saw my list and he ticked a couple. 'I will need four of your days,' he said. 'I need a strong man who can lift engines.'

I walked to the museum. It was closed for renovation. The curator of the museum was there.

'Anything for me?' I asked.

He scratched his head. 'There is always something for you. I need something moved, something heavy. Can you come tomorrow?'

'I can do it now,' I said.

'Sure, if you can.'

I bent my back, carrying a statue and a bell, precious remains of our town, shifting them from one room to another. In return, the curator gave me a sack of coal that was good to fire up an oven.

By the time I reached the police station, it was evening. I met the inspector. He tried to place me, and in the end, he thought I was someone else. He was a tradesman in uniform, and he could afford the one luxury that I would kill for one day. He was smoking a cigarette. I needed a smoke. It was a thirst, a hunger, a need without an adequate name. The inspector's eyes narrowed when he saw me staring. He waved some smoke my way.

'Take a deep breath,' he said.

'I need an agent,' I said. 'Active. One that would rise to the occasion.'

His eyes narrowed again. 'I do not have an assistant,' he said. 'Are you mocking me?'

'I need a fermentation,' I said. 'Active yeast, if you have. My mother needs to leaven some dough.'

He tapped his cigarette and was about to stub it out and then he looked at me. I took it gratefully and there was enough for a drag and a half.

'And how will you barter?'

I put my hand into my pocket and pulled out the packet. I placed it before him. I couldn't bear to look at it. It was my last packet of Marlboros.

'I thought you had given up smoking?' said the inspector.

'I have. I cannot afford it,' I said.

He took the packet and examined it. 'Any good?'

'Dry,' I said. 'Toasted tobacco.'

My last stop was at the bank. It was a small shed in an obscure lane, a perfect setting for furtive men. I left my goodies outside and entered. Inside, it was spare and clean. There was a single counter manned by a youngster reading a magazine. Behind him, seated at a desk, was the manager. I approached the window and filled a form.

'You have come for?'

'A deposit.'

'Your name and id?'

The manager came up and the two searched their forms.

'You have been here before, and...'

They ran through my previous statement.

'I am sorry,' said the manager. 'Your count has fallen.'

'I am not eligible?'

He shook his head. 'If it is any comfort, I can tell you that in general the sperm counts are down.'

I left the room empty-handed. I picked up what I had sourced from elsewhere and returned home for the night. My mother had turned in and locked her door. There were dried fruits and some nuts she had left on a ceramic plate. I needed something to drink. The pale colour from reused teabags. I could use that.

That night, there was a mother of all battles between cats and dogs. There was so little to eat that their owners had let them loose and they had become strays. The best-looked-after, the trained pups and obedient guard dogs, couldn't fend for themselves. It was bloody and very noisy. The violence was visceral. The animals shredded and ate each other. People almost died listening to the barking, the yowling, the screaming, the howling and the keening. The cats were winning the war without end and both sides were so ragged that the rats entered the fray. There were many of them and they were fearless. Rats had begun to eat wood, my mother said. Near the railway station, they were gnawing mortar.

I couldn't sleep. I stared at the wall in the dim light that filtered in through the curtain. I was hungry. I got up and hunted and I found a packet of seeds. A packet with no label. What seeds were these? A fruit perhaps or a vegetable. There was no soil where they could be planted. There was no time. I ate the seeds.

The next day I worked myself to the bone. I kept myself busy. Work filled my day, emptying time of its sinister purpose. By the day's end, I had done enough to get some coconut flour and some coconut milk.

As the light faded, I went for a walk, and as was my habit, I stood at a crossroads. It was quiet, empty and desolate. Gravel led into the distance, the path narrowing, and near the horizon, it took a turn past bushes and bramble. I stood there till my feet ached, I was rooted not by the vista but the faint possibility of meeting people from the other side. They are all dead, my mother kept insisting. An hour passed by and nobody appeared. They could not all be gone, I thought, they could not all be prey to some hungry parable.

I returned dragging my feet in the gravel, small stones entered my sandals. I remembered walking barefoot on the grass in our colony, marvelling at footprints that were temporary. I used to lie in the afternoon in the shade of a tree, on top of the hill where nobody went. The seasons were gone, their memory faint. The grass had disappeared and the last tree had fallen.

I reached home, lit a candle, wet my pencil with my tongue and drew. For some reason, I struggled with my imagination.

I looked for old photographs. I found some gelatin prints and the one I wanted. My childhood home and next to it a particular tree. I painted the scene using leftover tea and a few drops of my blood. Slowly, very slowly, the red turned to brown. It was magical.

'Have you got everything?' shouted my mother, the next morning.

'Why don't *you* go out and get something?'

'I am busy,' she said.

My mother darned clothes in her spare time. She yearned for new thread but there wasn't any. She reused thread. She cut the warp from old clothes and unravelled the weft. She was working on a pile that some Chinese family had given her. She was done with them. I took them with me and walked a couple of miles to a settlement where, in a small house, the family repaired shoes. I gave them the clothes and asked for a measure of forbidden. The lady smiled and disappeared. She brought a small packet of black rice. 'Boil it well,' she said. I said I wasn't planning to. 'Then?' Bread, I said, my mother is going to challenge herself and make black rice bread. 'Why?' I thought for a bit. Why indeed? Because I am tired of eating shit, I said, and she is tired of writing fiction. 'You might need this,' said the lady, 'here, take this.' She gave me some precious edamame seeds. And a few drops of soya sauce.

We baked the bread, my mother and I, and the smell was so heavenly some neighbours arrived. We sat together and my mother made small portions. My taste buds opened; my eyes watered.

'What does it taste like?' asked my mother.

'An emperor's repast,' I said.

After the guests left, I cleared the table and sat with her. She looked happy.

'This is no longer a cruel world,' she said. 'People are nice to each other.'

'Hmmm,' I said.

'We say yes more easily,' she said, 'and take no for an answer.'

I grunted.

'Ask for help when you need something,' she told me, 'just like others do.'

'I will,' I said.

I did not need to. It was the age of barter. It was my time because the better part of labour was working with one's hands.

'No regrets,' said my mother. 'Right, son?'

'Yes,' I said. 'No regrets.'

She spent the evening cutting the warp. Tomorrow would unravel the weft.

THE ACCOUNTANT

The day began at 6 a.m. After eight hours of sleep, I awoke with no feeling in my left arm. I pulled in my feet and pushed myself up. With a click or two, my spine assembled. I walked carefully towards coffee. Coffee was dark roast heaped into a filter, boiled water poured to the rim. After a couple of sips, my eyes opened. I finished my tumbler and stared out of the kitchen window. I had trouble blinking.

I heard my sister stir in her room. She separated from her husband a decade ago and has been staying with me since then. She entered the kitchen, drank a glass of water, tied her hair and left to wear her shoes. We walked towards Birla Mandir. The street that leads to the temple was being swept of leaves. The morning air was pleasant, the sky a clear blue, as we neared the temple rose. We sat near the entrance on a public bench and we watched people carry offerings inside. We saw them leave. When the crowd thinned, we returned, walking slowly. The sun was still casting shadows.

We did nothing that day other than eat, drink, read, speak a few words and sleep.

This was precious, precious beyond words, the fact that I was free and feckless. It was a working day and it was within my rights to do what I pleased.

SOME YEARS AGO

My cousin Krishna was younger by a few years. He had joined a start-up enterprise in Bangalore. The fledgling company had very few employees, the average age of the promoters was just 28, yet their hairlines had receded. Their business plan was a pursuit of eyeballs. In 24 months, they captured a million. This way they had obtained funding. Krishna and I led parallel lives; I liked to believe they intersected when he visited me.

The night he came, there was a thunderous clap, and when I rushed to my bedroom window, there were sparks. The transformer had blown again. A hush descended over the locality. In the living room, my cousin was on his machine and the screen light gave his hair a glow. He was programming, with a cup of coffee by his side. His phone pinged now and then, emitting a white light with the frequency of a lighthouse. He looked up and stretched his arms wide, stood up on his toes and stretched again.

'What time is it?' he said.

We stood in the balcony with fresh coffee, warming our palms. The deep night was giving way to morning. It was still and very quiet. People were still asleep.

'Babu,' he said.

I placed a hand on his shoulder.

'I have been confirmed,' he said.

I was struck by a pang of jealousy. It hurt to think of what his take-home pay might be. Technology companies were generous paymasters, their generosity stoked by their high attrition rates.

'Your father would have been proud,' I said.

Krishna's father was the epitome of middle-class sensibilities. He had stuck to a job for thirty years in a nationalised bank. In all those years, he never celebrated a promotion or an increment. Those things happened quietly. He never discussed rising prices or complained about traffic. He did not smoke, he did not drink. He had two children, one boy and one girl, Krishna and Neha, and both studied in the school he had gone to, a local school that remembered him. It was a strict school that produced engineers, doctors and a small number of failures. Neha, a cheery soul, was one of their failures. She wanted to be an aerobics instructor.

Krishna was bright, smarter than me, an achiever. He topped his exams, borrowed money, went abroad to a great university and returned with an MS degree and a dollar loan. He did this on his own without thinking twice. His favourite phrase was 'the irony is'. Against advice, he spurned jobs from tech giants and joined a new outfit. I had asked him if he worried about his company's longevity, his own precarious position, his unforgiving loans and his monthly rent. And he said, 'The irony is, I feel secure.'

We were quite close in our teenage years and I remember going out with him to a music performance where a bunch of college kids wrestled with electric guitars and broke the stage. I never got to know his father very well. I might have if he had stayed alive. His mother and I had a strained relationship. I found her off-putting and I think she disliked me. I would ring the doorbell; she would open the door. There are ways of opening an entrance door. She had mastered one where our eyes did not meet, I was let in without a word, and as I walked down the small corridor, I felt unwelcome. I liked my cousins enough to put up with this undercurrent.

'He is in his room,' she would say, as I walked past.

When I came on hearing the news of her husband's passing, she said the same thing.

'He is in his room.'

He was lying on his side, his back to the door. I had to turn him over to see him properly. She helped me. He was stiff, heavy as a log, we grunted, and he fell onto his back. His eyes were open.

We stood for a while looking at him.

'I called you first,' she said. 'I knew you would come.'

Krishna was abroad, studying, and Neha was trekking in the Himalayas.

'What happened?'

'Nothing,' she said. 'He just turned to his side when I asked him a question and did not respond.'

I tried not to smile. 'A question?'

My uncle was a cussed fellow who spoke very little. Yet his mouth was his principal source of expression. He could express quite well his feelings of distaste without speaking. I thought if he smiled occasionally, everything would have been different. Why didn't he?

'The fact of the matter is,' she said.

He is dead, she meant.

The door opened and closed endlessly that day. The bell rang itself hoarse till I left the front door open. A pile of footwear formed outside. Some incense sticks were lit, garlands were formed, an old photograph surfaced, and from time to time, a few tears were shed. There was a sickly-sweet smell that gave me a headache. Somebody had closed his eyes, but he was still peeping out of his lids. Nobody could straighten his mouth.

'If you ask me,' she said.

They were enquiring about his last wishes. As if he knew he was dying. He didn't. He wasn't unwell, not that we knew. He hadn't made a will, nor did he discuss last rites as I knew some in our family did. There was this ghoulish satisfaction they had in discussing what they wanted done.

'Cremate me nearby, and electric please. It should be quick. Don't you dare break my head, even if the panda insists. Take my ashes in a pot to Varanasi to a clean ghat, it should be morning, pick a nice boat, wait till you get away from the shore, and when no one is looking, spread them gently on the water along with flowers and one lamp. Don't dump them.'

My uncle was hoisted onto a rickety cart, cotton stuffed up his nostrils. He went in a jolly procession to a nearby crematorium. Krishna and Neha arrived just in time. It was a traditional cremation. We burst crackers on the road, a few boys danced, they lit him up and they broke his head. And when his gathered ashes came, we went to a nearby tributary, threw his remains over our shoulders and walked away, never looking back.

We asked her later. She said so many things. I looked at her in wonder. The fact that she could speak whole sentences, that she could reminisce.

'Keep the day's newspapers,' I said.

There was no other way of remembering that day because the rest of what happened you wanted to forget.

She went through his papers and I sorted them out. I arranged everything in piles, then rows, then files, and finally, I tore up what wasn't required. We looked at the four files at the end of the day and they stayed that way for a week. I thought I should give her some advice. I assumed she might be at a loss.

'Take some time off,' I said.

'From?'

'Just go,' I said. 'Wellness camp, 360-degree nature, Ayurveda massages. Go to a spa. Don't think about anything.'

'I need to lose weight,' she said. 'Weight gathers where you don't want it to.'

'I see.' I tried not to look. The fact of the matter was she was fine.

I returned to Delhi. My sister searched my face and found it troubled.

'What?'

'I believe there were more people at his funeral than at his wedding,' I said.

'You are a small man,' said my sister.

People call me Babu, a respectful greeting in some circles, a colloquial term for a government servant. It is also my name. I worked in the Accountant General's office in a soulless building, and at a relatively young age, my skin lost colour and I developed a slight stoop. My sister called me out. She said just look at you. I wore grey pants, black shoes and white shirts. In winter, I wore a grey half-sleeve sweater and a grey cap. Most days, I sat in the office and pushed files.

After five years, my sister said, 'Let me know when you are bored.' When ten years passed and I was still where I was, she said, 'How can you get used to this?'

I did not have such questions. My life was simple, it wasn't bleak. I was biding my time. I was focused and tenacious, and I had a quality my future boss described as innate suspicion. After a decade, I was shifted to forensics. My life changed.

A government car came to pick me up every working day. My new office had powerful computers, it had retained software companies to mine data and breach security walls. I carried my lunch to the office in a steel box and some water in a thermos. I moved into government quarters. They were modest but centrally located. I stayed alone, I never married, and though I had been with women, they never moved into my place. Government quarters were off-putting. There was no by-law against live-in relationships but nobody dared.

I spoke once at the India International Centre. There were thirty people in the audience that dreary afternoon. My topic was accounting skulduggery.

I introduced myself. 'I am a forensic auditor,' I said. 'In another world, I would be called a detective. The world of accounting is quiet; nobody notices what happens day-to-day. Times have changed. What happens in accounting affects share prices and drives values. Today, more than ever, there are criminal masterminds and there are suspense accounts. Accounting is supposed to be conservative; measurement is supposed to be honest and exact. We are not supposed to interpret things or exercise our discretion. You might ask me, how come there are so many scandals? You see, there are some amongst us who are willing to create fictitious entries, who wish to assist dishonest promoters and enhance their personal wealth. For such people, we have created a department of forensics. This unit chases these fictions, uncovers these adjustment entries and that dreaded black hole called "a suspense account".'

My assignments made me cynical. Uncovering wrongdoing was a thankless task. The first few successes gave me a thrill, thereafter I began to hate these people who went to such great lengths to beat the system.

Neha came by to Delhi for a holiday, to meet friends.

'You have changed,' she said. 'You seem to have aged.'

She wanted to learn how to drive a car. I was supposed to teach her and what I had was a government car, which was an Ambassador. She complained, said it did not look nice for her to be seen in one, even if it had a flashing red light that gave her right of way.

'The car is so bulky,' she said. 'The gear doesn't engage, and in neutral, it rattles.'

'Have you seen the boot?' she asked. 'The two of us can sit in it and share a light.'

She smoked like I did. We sat in the open boot and dangled our legs. She inhaled, puffed her cheeks, and then looked at me from the corner of her eyes and burst into laughter. I envied her future husband.

'For the record, I haven't aged,' I said.

There were three of us in the Special Investigation Unit (SIU). Besides me, there was my boss, and above him the head of the unit. We served in the Indian Accounts and Audit Service (IAAS) which was a notch or two below the Indian Foreign Service (IFS) and the Indian Administrative Service (IAS). IAS and IFS were premium cadres. But as part of the SIU, we had their respect because we could hold them to account. When tricky questions were asked in the Parliament, when committees were formed to investigate past actions and when politicians had an axe to grind and needed some dirt, they came to us.

We were vultures. We had the patience, the talons and a firm grip on the prey. We could not be shrugged off. Despite my special skills and predatory power, I received no special treatment. My pay scale was normal, my perks were simple. I stayed in a modest two-bedroom apartment in Mandir Marg, near an old bazaar called Gol Market.

Krishna was making more money in a month than I was in a year. I began to dread his visits. The last time he came, he bragged about his recent acquisitions. When he looked around at our possessions, sitting in our living room, my sister and I cringed. Concessional shopping was what balanced our budget. There was a rogue called inflation that kept creeping up on us, eating into our savings. A cheap shadow loomed over us when Krishna visited.

'You need to loosen up,' Krishna said. 'You are so stiff all the time.'

'My back is acting up again.'

'Why? What is there for you to worry? You don't need to provide for anybody.'

I bit my tongue. 'I need to make amends,' I said.

'For what?' He looked around pointedly. 'You haven't done anything so far.'

'Make amends for what I am going to do,' I said.

'Seriously?'

'Yes. There are too many people making money too easily. The system is rigged. It is up to me to set things right.'

He laughed. He had questions and he had come to me for answers.

'They are planning to give me stock options,' he said. 'I am getting them for a pittance. It is a huge amount in terms of market value.' He dropped his voice. 'I am a potential multimillionaire, but nothing to show right now, mind you. HR told me they have a crafty method to evade tax.'

I kept my counsel.

'I have no clue about shares and the market,' said my cousin. 'Should I take up these stock options? Could you analyse my company and advise me?'

'Give me some time,' I said.

My sister and I had a strict upbringing. Our mother died when we were in our teens. Our father made an example of himself, and in his later years, I thought he put on a show just for us. He was scrupulous to a fault. 'No favours,' he would say, wagging his finger. 'Not now or ever. Do not take any favour from anyone even if they are family and especially from your friends.'

He was so rigid it was ridiculous. What were family and friends for, anyway?

By age twenty my sister and I were done with studies and employed. By twenty-five we should have been married. My sister succumbed but I held out. My sister's marriage failed and she got a divorce. I remained a bachelor. I was in between relationships when she moved into the spare room in my modest abode. Our father sulked, long distance. He refused to travel to Delhi to meet us.

Meanwhile, the Indian Renaissance was in full swing and spending was the new mantra in every Delhi locality. Malls were the salons of the new Indian summer. Kitsch was the new aesthetic. A new car was launched every month, a new housing development leapt at you from every hoarding, and a brand ladder was being built for shirts, suiting, party dresses, toys, laptops and phones; rungs were getting added every day. The climbing never ceased. We were exposed, my sister and I, resisting, wrestling with this futile notion that we did not have to keep up with anybody in the sweet little city called Delhi.

I sit in a steel chair in an office amongst immovable objects that embrace inertia and fight velocity. I have seen people reduced to tears. Some have progressed to threats. The more sensible ones have tried to cajole us, pleaded their case and ended with entreaties. This emotional parade feeds my ego and keeps me sane. I am a small man as my sister says.

The first lesson in our bureaucracy is that nothing is as powerful as an immovable object, especially when people are willing it to move, with all their might, and these are powerful people who are unused to being rendered impotent by a junior officer.

The office does not allow me to be spontaneous, it discourages invention and daring. The dullness of routine and the woodenness of procedure have been laid down since colonial times ostensibly to keep us honest. They have gone overboard; they have leeched the discretionary from day-to-day happenings. All we have to do in office is subsume ourselves.

In a good bureaucracy, rules and regulations and the files that contain them have a negative energy. Each file is connected to others that precede it, succeed it or coexist with it. This network is called a matrix. Many people of intelligence have spent their lifetimes constructing this matrix and over the years it has taken over from them, and us, and today it is a Being. Some days I can see the matrix, just as a musician can see a raga. I can see its complexity and its magic.

A matrix of rituals and beliefs led me to religion. I had a large pantheon to choose from. I was led, I believe, by who I was—a small man wishing to fit into a larger purpose, willing to undergo personal pain—to the monkey god, Hanuman. Hanuman ji was preferred by bachelors, being one himself. I was in love with the many forms of Hanuman ji and I travelled to places far and wide to discover a different rendering. I read books that eulogised Hanuman ji. I feel I got to know him, what he stood for. I got from him my devotion to work. I owed him the strength of my beliefs. I could visualise being like him, setting my tail alight, so I could burn down an enemy kingdom like he did Lanka.

Other than Hanuman, there was another in my personal pantheon. I worshipped the lord Bhairava. There was a temple in Kalkaji that I visited every week. Bhairava is a manifestation of Shiva, the fierce one. He is the guard, the one who supposedly protects people from greed and lust, a particular duty in the times I live in.

My sister does puja every day. Her puja sthal is a small corner. It is personal and intimate and, in its vicinity, I am an intruder. She asks questions of deities, she speaks to them, leaves offerings like flowers and fruit, and she shuts her eyes for as long as it takes for bhakti to recede. I like watching her pray. She has a bath, she wears kumkum on her forehead and fresh clothes, and she gets into the zone. I recede from her consciousness. The locality is noisy in the mornings, but for a few minutes, she is oblivious. I envy her.

My worship is different. I don't ask for anything, but I like to see physical evidence. The temple matters, the idol matters, the ritual is important, the flame has to be felt, the offering has to be purchased, the priest has to be impressive, the chant has to be sublime.

'You were to advise me,' said Krishna.

He wouldn't go away. He had brought his company's annual reports and I had perused them carefully. I was truly amazed at the growth that his company had achieved and the margins they were making.

'Have you read these financial statements?'

'I tried but gave up,' he said. 'But I do know that our profits are good, fantastic actually, our growth is stellar, and we are potentially a stock market darling.'

I opened the Annual Report, got to the Balance Sheet and stared at the Reserves. They were humungous. I looked at the Cash and Bank balance. Surprisingly small. I had delved into the Receivables, a place where companies normally fiddled—inflated receivables often meant cooked-up sales. The Receivables were higher than the average.

'Are you losing people?' I asked. 'Are your employees getting poached?'

'All the time,' he said. 'Our attrition rates are very high.'

I turned the pages and got to the Income Statement. I pointed my finger at it.

'It tells you what happened during the year. Whether you made or lost money.'

'Any problem?' he asked.

There was so much I could tell him. 'The devil's in the detail, in the aggregation of a million transactions, thousands of vouchers and hundreds of ledgers.'

'It is all computerised now,' he said.

'Yes. The entries are captured. But at the origin, it is all paper.'

'A mountain of paper?'

'Literally. Pen and ink, printouts, tabulations, box files. Fodder for thieving accountants and silverfish.'

'You are so cynical!' he said. 'How come?'

'Good question,' I said. 'I am a pugmark tracker. I follow spoor, in this case, the number trail and the paper trail. I focus on fast-growing, profit-spewing companies like yours. Come to think of it, your company is a good case study for our unit.'

'What do you do in your unit?'

'In SIU, we are sniffing dogs.'

'You are an investigator?' asked Krishna. By now some alarm bells were ringing in his head.

'Yes,' I said. 'I am a forensic investigator. I am after those who believe in God and commit financial crimes.'

'What?'

'These people are believers. They believe they will not be caught. These are intelligent people, like you, a little too intelligent perhaps. They are always surprised when we uncover their wrongdoing.'

Krishna looked a little nervous. 'Listen,' he said, 'forget I asked you anything. I had no idea you spent your time chasing dirt.'

'I do,' I said. 'I don't mind saying so. There is a peculiar and unexplained pleasure in dirt being uncovered. You must have had the same feeling discovering the snot in your nose, the wax in your ear, the dirt in your belly button, the hairball behind the almirah.'

'You are a strange man,' said my cousin.

I had many arguments with my boss. He was a humid fellow who sneezed often into his hanky. His shirt had sweat patches, and by afternoon, he was a magnet for flies. The unit knew when he had worked on a file because the ink would be smudged on many pages.

'I can trace the origins of the decline of capitalism,' I said.

My boss grunted. The grunt meant he was half-listening.

'I am not a professor of anything, but I am a keen observer of human nature and a student of nifty accounting.'

'You are in my office,' said my boss, 'not in the India International Centre.'

'You want to know where the crime begins?'

'Crime?' He looked up.

'We created the idea of a company as an artificial person, a separate entity from those that set it up. This company gets a name and has a life. Its lifeblood comes from capital contributed by the owners—we will call it equity. We have allowed owners to break this equity into small units and, horror of horrors, we allowed them to buy and sell them.'

'That is called the capital market,' said my boss.

'A market where owners can sell up to seventy-four per cent of the capital, make more money than the company itself and still remain owners.'

My boss was mildly puzzled. 'Isn't the capital market the driver of capitalism?'

'The capital market has become a casino.'

'There are controls, Babu,' said my boss. 'There is regulation.'

'Yet the markets have collapsed time and again. When will we learn?'

'What is there to learn?'

'That this is a form of virtual reality, where earnings have fictional multiples, everything is leveraged, and in no time, a house of cards has come up where there was a small shelter.'

My boss looked worried. 'Are you turning socialist? You need to calm down.'

'I am calm, sir.'

'Are you suggesting no more capital markets?'

'Yes.'

'Then where will greed go? How will we grow and feed the millions?'

'We should collapse these markets,' I said. 'They are on steroids. And they are based on suspicious and inflated numbers.'

'The market is the present value of all our tomorrows,' said my boss.

'Capitalism will collapse soon,' I said. 'The big collapse is coming and we have only accounting to blame.'

'You mean lax accounting?' That was his favourite topic.

'Accountants these days bend backwards to please the owners of the capitalist machine.'

We went back to work after my tirade. We were examining employee stock option programmes (ESOPs) of software companies. These companies were enjoying huge valuations. Some of them had questionable accounting practices. They were inflating earnings, their stock prices were zooming, and fake promoters and their employees were cashing in. Our unit was tasked with exposing them all. We were after one large firm that was a serious cause for worry.

I wanted to take down these companies. Each and every one of them. My boss said my zeal was evangelical. He hated fervour in office. We are not vigilantes, he said.

'A man came from a big five accounting firm,' I said.

'Four. Big four. There are only four now.'

'Four then. He was a foreigner, could be American because he spoke loudly and he used a phrase.'

'What phrase?'

'He said, I don't give a rat's ass what you think.'

'And what were you thinking?'

'Does it matter? I haven't seen a rat's ass. Have you? No, I am just joking. But he wasn't. He meant what he said, every word.'

'He was here to check on your work, right? He was here to audit your audit?'

I nodded. He had come on behalf of a client, a fund that had invested in the large company we were investigating, and the fund was worried that the file was with the SIU. That bit of news had sent the share price southward.

'And you cooperated with him? Fully?'

'Of course. I had no choice. I had clear instructions from the super boss, in writing. I was to provide whatever information he needed, answer all his questions to the best of my ability and when appropriate say, I don't know.'

'And did you give a rat's ass what he thought of you?'

The fact of the matter was, I did. He thought I was incompetent and he said so.

'Is the company guilty?' he had asked. 'Yes or no?'

'We are not sure,' I said.

'You have taken so much time and you have no proof. The needle of suspicion is killing this company. My fund has invested a billion dollars in it. You should close the file.'

'I cannot,' I said.

It seemed a contiguous event when three suits from the private sector came to my office. The private sector came in suits, winter or summer, rain or shine. The cut of the private suit was elegant, almost severe. The three of them dropped pleasantries and tried to be jovial. And then they asked me if I knew what a Trojan was.

'A horse?'

'A Trojan is an implant,' one of them said, 'an intelligent drone.'

They gave me their visiting cards. They were from the large software company that we were investigating, the one that was a stock market darling. It had leapt out of the woods in the last five years and shimmied up the valuation chain.

'We have come regarding a file,' they said.

'I understand,' I said. 'Your file is with me. It is safe.'

'You don't understand,' said one of the suits.

They slipped me a handwritten note that had a number. I had a giddy spell looking at the zeroes. These were hard-headed business people, crude by nature, base by instinct, masters of quickly conveying the essence. I was meant to do their bidding, succumb to the money they were offering. All they asked of me was to bury their file in the almirah in our office. I tore up their piece of paper and asked them to get lost.

'Fair enough,' said one of them.

'Respect!' said another.

They went away, smiling, more than a little cocky.

For the next month, I went to work with a vengeance, auditing their records. I was desperate to find out how these suits were cheating the system. After spending thirty days, I had uncovered nothing. Their method eluded me. My boss joined me in my efforts and after a week, even he was baffled. For the first time, our unit faced defeat. I was distraught and it affected me so badly that I fell sick. My boss tried to counsel me.

'You are intelligent, Babu, but your ego is fragile,' he said. 'It is not a good combination.'

'What are you trying to tell me, sir?'

'Don't do anything foolish,' he said.

I called the suits and said I would change my mind. On one condition. 'No money,' I said. 'Just show me how you have done it. I promise you I will bury your file.'

They discussed my offer among themselves. To my surprise, they agreed. 'We trust you, only you,' they said.

I visited the accounts office of the software company. I was introduced to one of the kids from the tech team. He claimed he did not understand accounting.

'Imagine a reliance on machines to do your accounting work,' he said. 'These machines use software, and this software is developed by a reputed German company. Everybody uses it. It is a large system with numerous routines. The number-crunching is a distance away from direct human supervision. So much happens now in what we call the black box.'

'Be specific,' I said. 'What exactly do you do?'

'I infiltrate the subroutines of the accounting software. I plant Trojans in these subroutines. What happens is breathtaking. I am given the desired end results that the company wants that will take their share price up. And I am given the input numbers which they have actually achieved. Without my intervention, they will not get those end results. Guess what, because of my infiltration, despite the poor input numbers, the software produces the desired end result.'

'How do you evade detection? The intermediate workings will expose you.'

'My Trojans sense when someone is looking. They create a layer where intermediate workings get adjusted on a dynamic basis.'

I tried to understand that.

'If anyone were to slice the numbers, they will get the correct intermediate results.'

'If anomalies are spotted, then what happens?'

He smiled. 'This does happen. Then the Trojans intervene, the numbers move and the anomaly disappears. Mind you, I can only do this with large companies and big data.'

I was probably open-mouthed by then. There was more. One of the suits spoke up.

'The idea that "states" change when observed comes from physics, from quantum theory,' he said. 'Ergo Schrodinger's cat. Ergo waves of sound whose behaviour changes once they are monitored. Sexy isn't it that sound waves sense they are being monitored and they behave differently? So fucking heady!'

When I returned to Delhi, I thought I was running a low-grade fever. My sister sat me down. I was getting dizzy spells. I was disquieted, numb and very confused. I had this premonition that what I had done would be recorded somewhere. My visits to the software firm, the audio files, the offer the thugs had made, my initial refusal, my subsequent offer and their acquiescence. All of this damning evidence would be there, residing in the cloud, on computers that stood in rows in farms in some desolate building.

'You are so warm, but your temperature is normal,' said my sister.

'Something is wrong with me,' I insisted.

She looked at me and smiled. 'I can see you are not feeling good. What do we do?'

After a couple of days, I was still feeling sick. She took me to a faith healer.

'Just get it out of your system. Knowing you, I have to tell you not to laugh.'

I was so dazed I went along.

The healer and her setting were comical. I tried hard to keep a straight face. It was a dark room and a strange tableau. She was older than me and she was dressed in a gown with many folds. Her curtains were brocade. The air was heavy, redolent of dated perfumes. She held my hand in hers and looked into my eyes.

'You have no idea what I am going to say,' I said.

'Just say whatever comes to mind.'

It was probably the right setting and the perfect audience for my rambling.

'This world I live in is unreal,' I said. 'My belief in the unreal began not with some Bollywood flick but with the real world in which there existed the real economy and the financial economy.'

'Go on.'

'The real economy dealt with tangible things, honest effort and hard-earned wages while the financial economy dealt with just pieces of paper that supposedly represented real things.'

'Like tarot cards? Sorry, just joking.'

'Those pieces of paper were a multiple in value of the real things they represented. Thanks to some lazy regulators, the financial economy is out of control, frightening and a real threat. The first paper was currency and it bought you value. This paper economy owns companies.'

'I see.'

'Now we have paper that sits on top of paper,' I said.

She said nothing.

'We call them derivatives. These derivatives are a multiple of what they sit on. These derived products have a life of their own. They have truly mutated.'

'I haven't seen a derivative,' said my faith healer.

'Most people haven't,' I said. 'It is unreal. In the beginning, they were created to manage risk.'

I started laughing and couldn't stop.

'Now they are the risk. That is the mutation, a 360-degree transformation, and we are all in deep shit. Risk was meant to be managed, now it is an opportunity. Risk is the mother of God, risk is everything, imagined and real, and risk will drive all of us to our prosperous graves.'

My faith healer had let go of my hand. 'Interesting,' she said. 'I like your passion. Don't lose it. Ever.'

'You look happy. How was it?' asked my sister, as we headed home.

In a curious way, it had been helpful.

I did what I said I would. The file went into the office almirah. It was the price that I had agreed to pay. The SIU closed the case. The company stock rebounded and did well for a year after that. In the meantime, we went after other companies and they were less savvy and we were able to expose their fraudulent accounting. The entire sector suffered and the stocks tanked. The company, the one I had let go of, was investigated once again. Nobody could crack their code. No blame could be pinned on me. I was safe I thought. And then the American returned.

I called him John Doe because he wished to remain anonymous. John Doe returned to India to dig my grave. That is what he said. He had spent six months with a bank of computers and had unearthed the devilish subroutines, the Trojans and the sensors. He confronted the company and made sure the entire top management resigned. Under interrogation, the three suits mentioned my name and the fact that I knew. The fund was livid. They informed my boss. And they sent John Doe to the SIU to help with my culling.

He arrived without fanfare and asked me if we had a meeting room or a conference room. I made room for him by shifting some files off a chair. He sat in it holding a briefcase in his lap, his spectacles hung on the edge of his nose, so he had to look up first and then at me. 'Okay,' he said, with a shrug. 'If this is the best you can do.'

'Coffee?'

'Do you have mineral water?'

He opened his bland briefcase. It had crisp latches that snapped open. He pulled out a used quarter pad, opened his fountain pen and tested it on the side of a sheet. I rearranged some miscellany on my table: a stapler, a glue stick and a pencil sharpener.

'Where is the file?' he said. I gestured to the almirah in the corner.

'Should I?'

He nodded.

My legs were leaden and my back ached as I rose and opened the almirah. The file was there. I brought it back to my table. John Doe took the file, placed it on his briefcase and flipped through the pages. Once he was done skimming, he closed the file.

'Damning,' he said, 'that you closed this file despite the grounds for suspicion.'

'The last time you came here you sang a different tune,' I said.

The questioning began.

'Why did you do it? Why did you allow them to get away?'

'My unit had to know how this company did what they did. It was important for us in the long term. We had to snare the other companies.'

He doodled on his pad. 'You knew you would be accused of being partisan?'

'Yes.'

'Did you take anything at all from them?'

'No.'

'They made an offer?'

'Yes.'

John Doe looked at me for a while. 'I can decode the most complex machines,' he said. 'I am having trouble with you.'

'I wish I could help you,' I said.

'I don't understand men who place their reputation and their career on the line for no good reason.'

'Don't think too much,' I said. 'I am a nobody.'

'You *were* a nobody,' he said. 'You were a small, obscure man till you played God.'

It was an analogy I could live by. It was time I said something.

'There were miscreants outside, John Doe,' I said, 'and I was living in a prison.'

He looked around him. 'It sure looks like a prison.'

'You will never understand, John Doe, what all of that meant for someone like me.'

'Good for you,' he said. 'You conducted your court for a few days. You brought down all those companies. You crashed the market. Was it worth it?'

'I am not sure,' I said. The big day had come and gone. I was left with a strange indifference.

He seemed dissatisfied with my replies. 'Are you hiding something?'

'No.'

'I could have you investigated, you know?'

'You should,' I said. 'You can stake out my entire life and you won't find a thing.'

He persisted. 'Something doesn't add up.'

He wanted me to explain myself.

'I must tell you, I asked around and found out where you live. I went to your place when no one was there. I wanted to check out if you really stayed in a shithole. You do. Your office here is another shithole. You really are the nutcase I thought you were.'

I had to get rid of him.

'My cousin Krishna, his father died some years ago,' I said. 'I went to Bangalore and met his wife and she couldn't complete a sentence. I went for his cremation where they lit him up and then broke his head. They call it Kapal Kriya. I saw it. I thought, one day they will do this to me. And then?'

'I see,' said John Doe. He shook his head. He absently picked up a small framed photograph from my table. 'What is this? A monkey?'

'No,' I said. 'Hanuman ji. Someone I revere.'

'A monkey god?' He smiled for the first time. 'Poor guy, his tail is on fire.'

I smiled as well. 'Indeed. He lit it himself. He had to destroy an alien kingdom. Anything else?'

I saw him to the door.

'What should I do?' he asked me. He was clearly offering me some leeway.

'Do your damnedest,' I said. 'I don't give a rat's ass any more.'

PENALTY

Daily quizzes and weekly reviews tethered Priya to her study table. The school was international, the class size was ten and what she got used to was undivided attention.

'She never strayed,' said her father, Alok.

'But she had mood swings,' said her mother. 'Ask me!'

Their daughter spent more and more time in her washroom with her headphones on. When they peeped into her room at night, they found their only child curled in a foetal position.

'Her friends in school,' said her mother, 'they shared lunchboxes and wrote each other's essays. Is that allowed?'

'In the end, it didn't matter,' said Alok. 'The essays were unreadable.'

Priya had barely finished school when Alok had her take a standardised test called SAT. It was a life event. Priya returned, sat in her washroom for a couple of hours, and emerged dishevelled.

'Can an elephant run zigzag?' she asked. 'Does a tiger eat grass?'

'No,' said her father.

'Then why would you herd them with the deer?'

'Beta, there is a cut-off in every admission test,' said Alok. 'No use complaining. Clear it and then you can run zigzag.'

'Why can't colleges interview me?' said Priya. 'How can they decide based on a two-hour test?'

'Don't argue with metrics,' said Alok. He was an engineer by training. He remembered fondly the Indian Institute of Technology entrance exam that he had passed in his first attempt. He had worn the IIT badge all his life.

Priya spent an hour with her mother explaining the evils of relative grading.

'The results are curved,' she said. 'You know what that means?'

'No, beta.'

'It means the deer that runs faster escapes the lion.'

'Your father is the lion?' asked her mother.

Alok spent a ton of money funding Priya's undergraduate programme in the USA. Priya insisted on a college on the East Coast, one that had a broad-based humanities programme. She returned, magna cum laude, a queen from the land of rhetoric.

Father and daughter could no longer have a simple conversation. There was a time when they sat for hours on a sofa, tissues by their side, watching sad romances and comedies with laughter tracks.

Alok's sister was learned, an Indian academic who understood what Priya was going through.

'It is a phase, Alok,' she said. 'Firstly, your poor girl suffered the baccalaureate programme, then an American humanities course. It is natural that her spirit will be rebellious and her spout will be postmodern.'

The poor girl had stress pimples and a minor squint.

'Blame it on rhetoric,' said Alok's sister. 'And the fact that she has read *The Bell Jar*, Margaret Atwood, and Sophocles.'

'Really? I mean you really think so, Aunty?' said Priya. 'Would you like to set the curriculum? Should I, like, read the Vedas to get clear skin?'

Priya was schooled among other things on inappropriate physical contact. Every time Alok tried to hug her, she reacted like a deer. His spoken English came under her scrutiny. She shredded his stock phrases. Most of what he said in normal conversation was politically incorrect.

'I thought words have simple meanings,' said Alok.

'There is something called context. You won't find context in a dictionary.'

'Fine, I won't look.'

'By the way, you are also gender insensitive.'

Priya's new wave of sensitivity was accompanied by a new wave of allergies.

'My friends are turning vegan. Some are gluten-free.'

The family diet was in a shambles. 'No kachoris, no croissants and no cheesecake.' She said yes to imported berries, soft cheeses, quinoa and oil pastas. In all this, her complexion ranged from bad to worse. She blamed it on her career, which she saw as an imposition. She wanted to work in a non-profit, she was drafted instead into the family business.

Priya maintained a journal in a black Moleskine notebook. She was careless with it, leaving it where Alok would find it. The journal became a means of communication. Alok was meant to read her ongoing conversation with life.

Dear Diary,
My father is going to die before me. These are the odds and I am going by them. I wish to prepare for this event. There is nobody who can help me. There is no anonymous group. Perhaps I should start one. The

reason I bring this up is that I am obsessed with this eventuality. I have no idea how I will behave when it happens. What will life be like without his presence?

Alok could not read further. He tried to imagine what her life would be like. He knew the man in her life, the young man she was seeing. His name was Arjun and he was, by common consent, a fine young man.

Priya asked him a series of questions.

'Is it true that when girls get married, they bid goodbye to their parents? Are we traditional that way?'

Before he could reply, 'Can you visualise my staying with my husband in your house? There is enough room. I would love that to happen.'

Alok was slow to respond.

'Don't bother replying. I know the answer.'

The journal disappeared for a few days and Alok did look around for it. One day it reappeared and it had some new entries.

Dear Diary,
I look at my father. He is in his sixties and has lost a few things. His back complains, now and then, and when it does, he is insufferable. He has right-hand orientation. He has played golf for a few decades. In each round, he probably stood a hundred times over the ball with his right shoulder below the left. I can see what this has done to his spine.

Alok straightened and felt his lower back.

I am like him, a golfer, prey to the habit, a resident of a small universe that prides itself on spending hours in a special solitude. My father says the golfer's way is a coda, a way of life. We are servants of fair play, he says, we are gentlemen.

He complained of breathlessness one day and we rushed him to a hospital. As he lay on the hospital bed, looking vulnerable for once, he spoke to me about legacy.

'You are twenty-eight years old,' he said. 'You should handle the family business.'

'I am not ready,' I said.

'What?'

I said, 'I don't have a designation, no fixed working hours, I come and go as I please, nobody kicks my arse and yet every month I receive a fat salary.'

'Have you learnt nothing?' he asked.

'You have put me on a pedestal,' I said. 'I can't handle shit.'

I was depressed. I needed professional help.

He said, 'Analysis is a fancy import, good for foreigners with broken families. We Indians don't need it.'

Duh.

On occasions like these, he is my pet hate.

Alok dissuaded her.

'There are times when exercise helps. Hit the road, run a few kilometres every day. Or join a gym.'

'And that will clear my head?'

The only way he could get her to join a gym was by sending her for a health check.

'I will go,' she said, 'just to prove you wrong.'

She went. She carried her reports to show them to Dr Muthukrishnan, a general practitioner and a friend of her father. He was holding her reports when she entered his fluorescent room. 'Do you exercise?' was his first question.

'I play golf, like my father,' she said.

'Alok didn't tell me. How much time do you spend on the course?'

'Five hours, if I am playing with somebody. Otherwise four.'

'And how many times a week?'

'Three,' she said.

'That's good. That's very good.'

'Mostly I play alone,' she said.

It sounded like a confession. It was one.

The doctor looked a little surprised. 'Just you?'

'Yes, me and my caddie. I was never into team games, so my father introduced me to golf.'

The doctor took out his blood pressure machine, an old-fashioned contraption.

'How can you play alone? Who are you playing against?'

'Against the golf course,' said Priya, as she rolled up her shirt sleeves. The doctor puffed the machine, the wrap tightened and Priya stiffened. 'And against myself. I play against my handicap.'

She eyed the liquid as it rose and fell. Her doctor compared the reading to the one in the reports and frowned. He wrote out a prescription.

'I am a high handicapper,' Priya heard herself saying. She was in full-blown confession mode.

He peered at her. 'You spend five hours thrice a week at something you are not very good at?'

She nodded. The doctor had no idea how much time she spent doing things she didn't like.

'You enjoy the outing, perhaps? Must be like a picnic?'

Priya massaged her forearms. 'I wish I could play better.'

'Your father wants you to?'

Of course, he did.

Doctor Muthu smiled. 'Your reports are better by the way. Well done. You know this reminds me of homoeopathy,' he said, 'about a course of treatment that is effective despite the lack of scientific basis.'

'What do you mean?'

'I would say that in the quest for health, golf is your placebo.'

Alok was happy golf was helping his daughter stay healthy. He had taught her the basics.

'Lesson one. It is all about muscle memory,' he said.

'Which muscle?'

'The brain, what else?'

'It's a funny game,' said Priya.

'Keep a still head,' shouted Alok.

She giggled. 'I am trying.'

They played many rounds together, but as she grew older, they got into arguments. She was beginning to take over from her mother. She wanted to run the home differently. She wanted Alok to get involved in things, like setting up a charity, making a will, sharing financial information, discussing property decisions.

'Don't interfere,' said Alok. He received a lecture on patriarchy.

'Know your register,' said Priya.

'Register?'

'Your tone changes when you speak to my mother.'

'You are worried about tone? Not what I say?'

'It is how you say it. You don't realise how entitled you sound.'

Alok arrived in Chennai for an important assignment—to meet Arjun, his prospective son-in-law.

'Spend a couple of days with him,' Priya had said. 'Keep an open mind.'

He had prepared an itinerary, which Arjun had gracefully accepted. The first evening they went to an art gallery, a familiar haunt for Alok. He was a collector of sorts, in love with the art world and the people in it. He thought they were naturals, different—unashamedly so. He told Arjun as much.

'What do you mean, natural?'

'Free of pretence and dogma,' said Alok.

'Really?' said Arjun. 'I thought the art world revelled in both.'

'There are those people. Priya follows them, I don't. She reads what they write.'

'Priya told me you only collected artists who had been eaten by worms?'

'They are called Moderns,' said Alok.

'Should I also buy a Modern?' Arjun was earnest. 'You could guide me?'

Alok led him to a work and they stared at it for a while.

'It is beautiful,' said Arjun.

'No,' said Alok. 'I keep telling gallerists not to show people stuff like this. This is conventional craft, believe me. In aesthetic terms, this is bling.'

Arjun looked at the price list. 'It is cheap.'

'Ha,' said Alok. 'Do not take what is cheap, and recent, unless you need the write-off.'

'I like it,' said Arjun. He bought the work. Alok looked on in dismay. He thought of calling Priya and complaining.

'This could be a waste of money,' he said.

'My money is tired,' said Arjun.

'Tired?'

'Fatigue. It comes from years of bearing interest.'

'Funny,' said Alok.

'I like giving it to people like this artist. A little could tip the balance in his life?'

Alok knew Arjun came from a wealthy family. Two generations ago his family had toiled. He was blessed, for he had inherited what had been well earned.

They moved from the gallery to a bar in a hotel. Arjun had a long discussion with the bartender and ordered an expensive whisky.

'Uncle, your family is from Delhi?' asked Arjun.

'Yes,' said Alok. 'Our ancestors established a jagir, built a small chalet in Old Delhi with high walls, verandas and walkways. Fruits fell from trees in our compound, flowers bloomed in cornices.'

'How romantic!' said Arjun.

'My grandfather, Dadu, set up a family trust with tough conditions. He made sure the next generations would have to toil for their money. He took his fortune with him when he died, in a manner of speaking.'

'My parents are different,' said Arjun. 'They worked hard all their life but they did not impose their work ethic on me. I am free to do as I please.'

He said it simply, without pretence.

Priya called late at night. 'So, what do you think?'

'I don't know,' he said.

'That's all you can say?'

'What do you want me to say? Frankly, I don't know enough.'

'What *do* you know?'

'I know his family's antecedents, his caste, his date and time of birth, the school he went to, the college he wasted time in. I have his astrological chart.'

'Already?'

'Your mother insisted. I had one made. I am sorry but she also insisted it be compared to yours. Do you want to know the result?'

'No, of course not!'

Alok could sense her anger. 'He has no strong likes and dislikes,' he said. 'He seems a little rootless, like your generation actually. You all seem to be floating in no man's land.'

'That is your first impression?'

'He seems like a nice chap,' said Alok.

'I can't marry nice,' said Priya. She sounded unhappy.

'I should hack his computer,' said Alok. 'And his phone. That's the only way of understanding you young people. Do you have his passwords? Does he trust you that way?'

'Have you been drinking, Dad? Call me tomorrow after your golf round. I need a yes or no.'

Alok did not sleep very well.

He knew his daughter was in love. He wanted to like Arjun and was willing to give him a fair chance.

Arjun's parents stayed in Coimbatore where they ran a spinning mill and they had a family home in Chennai in Nungambakkam where their son stayed. When Alok reached his place, Arjun could be heard shouting.

'Get me my bag.'

The house was an old one, a bungalow with a veranda in front that had low-slung cane chairs. The windows were painted green, the house a shade of cream.

Arjun emerged wearing a green T-shirt and fawn slacks.

'Uncle,' he said, holding out his right hand. He had a firm handshake. His man Friday brought out his golf bag and a trolley.

'This is Selvam. He is our family retainer. Selvam, this is Priya amma's appa.'

'Namaskaram, sir,' said Selvam. 'How is Priya amma?'

Arjun did some push-ups, some side stretches and a few squats.

'Selvam, where is my coffee?'

Selvam brought a flask. They went to a large SUV. The boot was the size of a small room. The engine came to life with a shudder.

Horses neighed as they entered the course. Arjun's caddie was waiting at the parking lot. His name was William. He was senior-most, an old-school type. Like some players from genteel backgrounds, he was fond of alcohol in the morning. He had the best read of the Gymkhana greens. He knew English and perhaps the British as well. He spoke like them.

Alok's caddie was Babu. He was middle-aged and wore spectacles. He examined Alok's clubs, tested one for heft and balance, and then rearranged them to his satisfaction. In his day job, he was a bus conductor. He helped Alok wear his shoes and tied his laces. Arjun looked on, raised an eyebrow and took a photograph with his phone.

'Uncle, you haven't said a word all morning.'

They went to the practice range. In between shots, Alok watched his young compatriot smash the daylights out of the golf ball.

'You are a long hitter, longer than most that I have seen.'

Alok had his job cut out. Age wasn't on his side. The handicap system was there to protect him but how was he to impress his prospective son-in-law? He had his share of wins in club tournaments. The family pretended to take care of the cups. Some were in a glass cabinet, some on higher shelves from where they occasionally glinted and some were in a tin trunk where sporting memory tangled with rust. All the runner-up trophies went into the bin.

Arjun watched Alok hit a few balls.

'Have you been to a gym, Uncle?'

'No, I haven't,' said Alok. 'I have a yoga regimen that keeps me going. My yoga guru says gymnasiums are for gorillas.'

Arjun laughed. 'Shall we hit the course?'

The Gymkhana course had no trees. The golf course was inside the circular horse racing track.

'This is a links-style course,' said Arjun, as they walked to the first tee. 'It has small greens, many traps and the rough is evil.'

'Two-ball today, master?' asked William.

He handed Arjun the driver, the longest club in the bag.

'Yes, William,' said Arjun.

Alok had brought his set for the round. His bag had light clubs with senior flex and large heads that were termed forgiving.

'Par four,' said Arjun. 'Stroke index 7. I give you a shot.'

'You are giving me just eight shots,' said Alok. 'You said ten yesterday at the bar.'

'Sir,' said Arjun, 'let us begin with eight, then we will see.'

The boy was unmindful of commitments made in a bar, thought Alok. He took a few gentle practice swings while Arjun vigorously swung his driver to and fro, stirring up the air. He teed up the ball, stood behind it, taking aim.

'Hit, master,' said William.

Arjun swung hard, the ball took flight, began curving right, way right, and with a brief flash of white, it disappeared beyond the racetrack.

'Out of bounds, master,' said William.

Babu bent low and teed up Alok's ball. Alok sent the ball down the middle of the fairway with an easy swing.

Arjun teed up again and blasted a drive down the centre. It was probably 300 yards long.

'Great shot,' said Alok. 'I could never do that.'

'Any fool can do it the second time,' said William.

'Thanks, William,' said Arjun.

They walked down the fairway.

'Aren't you going to retrieve the first ball?'

'It doesn't matter,' said Arjun.

When he reached his ball, Alok asked for a hybrid club and sized up the situation.

'Left to right wind,' said Babu.

The ball started left and stayed left, finding the greenside sand trap.

'Bad luck,' said Arjun. 'In this course, it is better to hit short of the greens.'

'I like to hit pin high,' said Alok. 'I like to attack the flag.'

Arjun looked hard at him as if to say that for a high handicapper, uncle talks a lot. 'And you are a good bunker player, sir?' he asked.

'Yes, quite good, because I am in there very often.'

Alok won the hole. They moved to the second, a par three which Arjun won by hitting his tee shot six feet from the flag. The third was a par five.

'You don't use golf shoes, Uncle?'

Alok wore special shoes. 'I have trouble with my feet,' he said. 'I lost two toenails in my left foot because the golf shoe was stiff and a little tight.'

'Too early to be losing nails,' said Arjun. He pulled out a packet of cigarettes and lit his first for the day.

'Must be a blockage in an artery,' joked Alok. 'Thank God I don't smoke.'

He duffed his drive, the ball sneaking into thick rough. Arjun hit a good one. Babu ran, the bag shaking from side to side. They found him searching, using a club to part the bushes. He froze suddenly. 'Don't come here,' he said.

'Why.'

'Snake smell,' he said.

'You can smell a snake?'

'Babu can, master,' said William.

'Cobra, six feet long,' said Babu. 'It has a particular smell. It comes out in the afternoon.'

There was a large anthill amidst the bushes. It looked like home. They stood around and stared, their ears straining to hear the dreaded rustle.

'Drop another ball, master,' said Babu. 'No need to take a risk.'

'Free drop?' asked Alok.

'Penalty,' said Arjun. 'As per the rules, it is a lost ball. You have to go back and hit again.'

'But the ball is there!' said Alok. 'We will surely find it but for the snake.'

'Sorry, Uncle. You have to go back and hit again,' said Arjun.

Alok had to retrace his steps, trudge 200 yards back to the tee box. He dragged his feet, visibly upset. He stomped onto the tee box, and without preamble, he took a wild swing at the replacement ball. He sent it into the same bushes where the snake supposedly resided. He walked up to where the others were waiting, smoke coming out of his ears.

'Your hole,' he said.

Babu, an experienced caddie, pulled out a packet of Electral from the bag, mixed it with cold water from the flask and offered it to Alok.

'Hot day, sir,' he said.

'Your daughter allows you to drink these chemicals?'

Alok did not reply. They played a few more holes. It was obvious Alok was going through the motions. He was losing badly. Arjun was laughing and chatting, seemingly oblivious to his situation. He even cracked a joke.

At the eighth tee box, he broached the topic.

'Priya will not marry me unless you say yes.'

'Yes, is easy to say,' said Alok. 'She likes you.'

'Sir,' said Arjun, 'she will not marry me unless you like me. So, I have to get to know you and vice versa, and we have to get along.'

'Which is why we are golfing,' said Alok.

They waited while Arjun lit another cigarette.

'I like your game, sir,' said Arjun. 'But I thought you would be more competitive.'

'Ha ha,' said Alok, still seething.

'Priya said you had fire in your belly.'

'She forgot weakness in the knees.'

They finished nine holes and Alok was five down at the turn. They took a break for refreshments at the tenth hole hut. Babu stood, picking his teeth, inviting conversation. In the course of walking nine holes with him, Alok had discovered he was a wise fellow. He claimed his years of bus conducting had taught him about human nature.

'I can spot a ticketless traveller from a distance,' he said. 'On the golf course, I can spot a cheat.'

His golfing knowledge was good. His read of the greens was uncanny, his understanding of Alok's game was almost sinister. Alok thought, this is a man I can trust for an honest opinion. Arjun disappeared into the washroom and he seized the opportunity.

'There is an old saying among golfers that you cannot hide who you are from a caddie. Would you agree?'

'Yes, sir,' said Babu.

'Does Arjun cheat? Did he ever?'

'No,' said Babu.

He looked long and hard at Alok, as if he was reading a green. They shared a cup of tea and Alok reflected on what Arjun had said. Where was the fire in his belly? Alok had planned to test the young man's mettle during the round and instead here he was, having thrown in the towel, busy sulking over an imagined insult. Over the second nine, his competitive instincts revived and he played better. He chipped away at Arjun's lead.

'What if you lose today?' he said when he was just two down with four holes to play.

Arjun shrugged his shoulders. He was testing the wind, throwing wisps of grass into the air.

'I will shake your hand,' he said.

'Against the wind, master,' said William. He handed Arjun a seven iron. Arjun hit the ball onto the green.

'I believe you tried turning professional. You were that good at this game. Why did you give up?'

'I wasn't enjoying what I was doing,' said Arjun. 'It felt like work. My parents egged me on, but I gave it up.'

'I see.'

'Uncle, I love this game, I love playing it. I realised one day I didn't *have* to be the best at what I did. I did not *have* to be better than others.'

Alok was disappointed with what Arjun had said. 'People dream of winning, of being the best,' he said. 'And look at you!'

'Yes, look at me. Such potential and all I do is play for fun. I am happy, Uncle. Some days I shoot level par, some days I have an incredible round shooting five under the course.'

'And when you watch the professionals on tour? Does something happen to you?'

'Not any more.'

'Seriously?'

Arjun smarted at Alok's tone. 'You find this hard to understand?'

Alok patted him on the shoulder. 'I just think that for somebody with your talent and physique, it is a hollow justification.'

He won two of the next three holes and they arrived on the 18th tee box with the score all square. William and Babu were on high alert. The close battle had enthused them.

'Do you only like winners?' asked Arjun, as they prepared to tee off. 'I mean are you partial to such people?'

He sounded vulnerable for the first time.

'Winning in business, at work, is like second skin,' said Alok. 'It has happened so often I take it for granted. Is winning important? You bet it is.'

'And what have you lost, sir, if I may ask?'

The question touched a nerve.

'I lost someone I loved dearly. The cruel truth is she is still alive and with someone else.'

'And she is not Priya's mother?'

'No.'

The honesty surprised Arjun. 'Wow,' he said.

The memory upset Alok's rhythm. He swung hard. The ball flew towards the out of bounds area, hit a picket fence and rebounded onto the fairway.

'Golfing gods,' muttered Arjun, as he stepped up to the tee.

William handed him a three wood. 'Hit fairway, master.'

It was an order. Arjun complied. His lithe physique was framed against the horizon, and Alok remembered the impossible coil and the wonderful release. The small projectile left them, soaring into the sky and landed 100 yards past Alok's ball.

As they walked down the fairway, Arjun asked, 'Is the caddie your servant?'

'Why do you ask?'

'You treat Babu like he is one,' he said. 'He ties your shoes, tees up your ball, marks it on the green and picks it from the hole. You should do all of that.'

'You sound like my daughter,' said Alok. 'You young people are so alike.'

What Arjun said wounded Alok, but he did not say anything. Was a bad back a sufficient excuse for privileged behaviour?

Alok's second shot came up well short of the green. Arjun had an easy second shot and Alok could imagine him landing the ball on the green and winning easily. Arjun stood over the ball, ready to play, and then rocked back on his heels.

'The ball moved,' he said loudly.

'Master?' said William.

'I said the ball moved. I saw it.'

'Did you address it?' asked Alok. 'I mean did you ground the club?'

'Yes, I did.'

They looked at each other.

'To be fair, I didn't see it move,' said Alok.

'I am sure, Uncle,' said Arjun. 'The maker's name has shifted.'

Alok was astonished the young man had declared a potential penalty on himself. He could barely conceal his admiration.

'What happens?'

'A penalty,' said Alok. 'One shot. Mark and replace.'

Arjun lost the hole and the match. The victory felt hollow and irrelevant. Alok was thrilled his potential son-in-law had policed himself by invoking a penalty. It was a noble gesture, rarest of the rare in times that had changed so much. It was quintessentially what golf was all about.

'I feel like calling my daughter,' said Alok. His mind was made up. He wanted to convey his good wishes to Priya. She did not answer his call.

After the round, Babu and Alok sat near the car while Arjun disappeared into the clubhouse for a bath. Alok heard a noise and realised that Babu was chuckling.

'What? Are you remembering some part of my round?'

'Sir, the ball did not move,' said Babu.

'What? Are you sure?'

Babu nodded. 'It did not move,' he said again.

'Then?'

'I don't know, master. I don't know why he did it.'

'Why did he? I mean why would he invoke a penalty on himself?'

Babu said nothing more. Alok's mind was awhirl. He believed what Babu said to be true. The wily fellow had a sharp eye.

'Was Arjun trying to...?'

Babu was holding a stick in his hand. As Arjun emerged from the clubhouse and walked towards them, he threw it into a nearby bush.

'Master, I smell a snake,' he said.

Grooming Asok

The Chief Executive Officer was in a mood after three Glen whiskies, each pour a golden inch. He was drumming his fingers on the table, his knees were knocking its legs.

'Can you feel it?'

His trusted underling, the Chief Technology Officer, sat still. 'Sir?'

House music was playing, a fancy light bulb was drawing patterns on the sofa.

'Drink up,' said his boss, raising his glass. 'A toast.'

They clinked glasses. What were they toasting?

'You know,' said the CEO, munching loudly on a gherkin, 'we are in deep trouble.'

He knew it. The CTO had guessed correctly. He grabbed some cashews. This was going to be a long sob session.

'Bloodletting,' said the CEO. 'Heads are going to roll.'

The CTO shuddered. Could this be it? Was this his handshake moment? His boss was staring into his glass at an insect that had fallen in.

'Our valuation has halved,' said the CEO. 'I need your advice. How do we recoup?'

The CTO breathed easy. 'We could cut some overhead, sir.'

'No! We need a total revamp. We have to break things down for value to emerge. We need to rebuild with broken pieces.'

Drink four arrived, a half-inch. As did a middle-aged man clad in jeans and a T-shirt. He was bearded and wore dark glasses.

'Meet our new hire,' said the CEO. 'A scientist. He is our Chief Ideas Officer.'

The bearded man sat wordlessly. He didn't shake hands. He looked to the barman and signalled. While his drink arrived, he turned to the CTO and spoke to him directly.

'What you have with you is sinking. You have dogs in your product matrix.'

'I see,' said the CTO, cut to the quick. 'That was electric, your assessment.'

'I am not blaming you,' said the newcomer. 'Tech businesses age like black holes. As they say in my community, you cannot negotiate with gravity.'

The CTO still bristled. 'Perhaps you have a solution already?'

'Artificial intelligence,' said the CIO. 'Not the regular stuff. The Corporation needs something dramatic. I suggest a bot that has a mind of its own. Can you visualise that?'

The image was a powerful one, a rogue program made of reckless bits and bytes. One that would morph, multiply, wreak havoc in places more dangerous than their imagination, like the real world.

'A rogue?'

'A human bot.'

A few minutes' silence ensued.

'Are you with me?' asked the newcomer.

The CTO nodded. 'Don't worry, Mr Scientist, I heard what you said. I will remember every word.'

The CIO laughed, sounding a little nasty. 'Five years from now, you will remember this in two different ways,' he said.

'What do you mean?'

'Five years from now, the Corporation will be manipulating your memory.'

'Wow,' said the CTO. The evening had got away from him. 'Should I go now and plug myself into a socket?'

The CTO was convinced their star techie, Asok, had a hidden ailment. There was a lot about him he did not like. The boy had his tics and he was a walking eyesore. Asok had the attention of top management. The Corporation had two thousand employees, yet the CEO knew Asok by name and had even observed him discreetly.

'Something is not right,' said the CTO.

'We need more than your glib assessment,' said the CEO.

Ace programmers had considerable leeway. The big problem with Asok was his way of working. He did not document anything. The head of Quality Control set up a meeting to escalate the issue.

Asok's defence was a familiar one. 'My programs work, don't they?'

It was true. His work was faultless.

'Yes, they do. But it is quality without control,' said the head of QC. 'Half my job is making sure that anyone can dig into what you have done and make changes.'

'And why would you need to do that?'

'Contingencies,' said the CTO. 'The whole damn Corporation is wired for contingencies—except your little island.'

Donkey work was what Asok hated. He was asked to explain his code in simple English and adhere to approved formats. He was impatient, his mind capable of intuitive leaps. His output was remarkable, sometimes unbelievable.

'Is he on narcotics? Check his room, someone.'

He had a cabin of his own that nobody had access to. When the door opened, an acrid smell emanated, the harsh smell of stale sweat and uneaten meals.

'He is clean.'

'The bugger has some form of neurosis. Don't tell me later I didn't warn you.'

The CIO examined Asok's appraisal report. 'Irregular work habits. Sporadic meals. Poor hygiene. Insolence. On the plus side, Asok is a worker bee. Work is his addiction. In his presence, the rest look like laggards.'

'I will take him in my team,' said the CIO.

Asok stayed at the rear of a building that overlooked the rear of another. Where he sat, he was juxtaposed with two monitors on either side of an actual window. Beautiful screen savers flanked reality, a close-up view of fat toilet pipes with a coupling in between. The coupling leaked, around it green moss had grown. On weekends, Asok stared at the pipes, at crows that perched on the coupling and pecked at leaking waste, at a small plant that had taken root where the crows had dropped a seed. He stared late at night on weekdays, his eyes red, his mind a pixel daze. Three coffee machines, three powders. A whistle-blowing cooker that he rarely washed. Plates made of paper, mugs with graffiti. Noodle cups that never seemed to satisfy his craving. A clothesline strung from the sill to the kitchen window held up his weekly wash. He wove his way through, picking and choosing, each day a random ride.

Near his house was a gaming studio. It had darkened glass. From outside, only silhouettes were visible. A portion of the studio was accessible, a portion was cordoned off for experienced gamers. People like Asok had a swipe card.

He entered unhindered and sat at a particular machine, one that he had named 'Buddy'. It was a powerful device, fit for NASA perhaps. He loaded a war game and he shot some people. He chose the highest bore, inflicting maximum damage. After ten minutes of mayhem, he tired of it all. He needed oxygen. It was 11 p.m., too early to turn in.

He spent time in a 24/7 gym. The treadmill was his steed. He attached the safety clothespin and began his routine. The setting was middle-aged. He was ashamed. He dreaded numbers that reminded him how unfit he was. The gym supervisor tried to up the ante. After half an hour, his sedentary pace flagged.

The mirror was his enemy when he dressed for work. The sun was harsh, the truth was painful. The code in his office was smart casual. Asok tried on a few things. A faint smell reminded him the cupboard needed to breathe. On the way to the office, a hoarding had a male model lounging on a bike wearing collegiate clothes. He dreamt of matching his lazy elegance. There were many geeks in the office who could. He envied them.

He parked his bike, secured his helmet and wore his dark glasses. He leaned before the rear-view mirror and brushed his hair. He was late, the lot was full. He could hear a hum as he approached the glass tower block. He swiped his card and entered, dreaming of Neo making an entrance in *The Matrix*. Two pings later he was on his floor. Cameras followed him as he reached his room.

'Govinda has come,' said somebody. The office twittered.

Asok was afraid of asking for sartorial advice. There was Leela. She was plump and she wore sarees, sleeved blouses and a large bindi. She looked homely.

She screwed up her nose when he approached.

'Underarm,' she said. 'Smell.'

There was more. There was a scratchy feeling in his underpants. His tight pockets impeded his search. Leela noticed the salt-encrusted creases on his jeans. Nobody had died of poor hygiene in Chennai but many friendships had suffered.

'You lack confidence,' she said when he had pleaded his case. 'It shows.'

'I go to the right stores but buy the wrong clothes,' said Asok.

'Happens,' she said. She noticed his bulging eyes. 'Forget this business of good taste. Authenticity is what you need. Don't try to be like someone else.'

'How?'

'You have to find yourself,' said Leela.

She took him by the arm to a coffee shop. She told him who she was, where she came from. She spoke without inhibition. Asok was not sure why she was confiding in him. What was she hoping to achieve by spilling all those private details?

'Now you speak,' she said. 'Just like I did.'

'I came to college by mofussil bus leaving behind aged parents,' he said. 'I looked poor and rustic.' Then he stuttered. 'They called me a k-k-k-kattan.'

'Ragging?'

'Yes. Whenever they felt like.'

He showed her an old photo. 'When I joined the Regional Engineering College in Trichy.'

'So earnest!' said Leela. 'You were a topper?'

'Yes. I topped BTech, in computer science, then MTech.'

'Go on.'

He couldn't. She thought she should needle him. 'Some people in the office think you are mad. Do you know that?'

He shrugged.

'Talk to me about how you code. How you do your magic.'

Asok came to life. His face lit up, his eyes widened and his fingers played an imaginary piano.

'Usually, there is some music playing. Good code can be set to sound.'

He saw her smiling. 'I am serious,' he said. 'I write pure code. For that, you need a good ear. I programme like a musician visualises a raga, the big picture constantly in my head. The rest is engineering. The right skeletal structure and the wiring.'

He looked at her.

'You are making sense,' she said.

Reassured, he carried on. 'I pray a lot,' he said.

Leela looked surprised. 'Why?' she asked.

'When I code well, I become aware of a greater being,' said Asok. 'When I am done, I feel close to this being. You think I am mad?'

'What? No, of course not.'

'I pray to Murugan. We have things in common. We do the same work. We bring things into this world, things of great beauty.'

He thought of the leaking toilet pipes, the plant that had taken root in the muck, its first flower that had bloomed the very morning.

Leela was laughing. 'Sorry,' she said. 'You look so serious. I thought you were joking.'

Asok was hurt. 'I am serious,' he said again. His voice dropped. 'I haven't said this to anybody, but if you think deeply, like I do, you will realise that God belongs to artificial intelligence.'

'Err what?' said Leela. 'You lost me there. But it doesn't matter. Tell me more about your work.'

'First, they give me specifications, a document that tells me what is needed, and nothing else. I read it till that document possesses me. I am visualising a lot lately. It helps me cut out errors. Errors are painful, like getting hurt. I feel like I am bleeding when I see a mistake.'

'The next stage?'

'Next is what people call grunt work. I don't do that. I write arguments. Construct routines and subroutines. There are loops, gates... you know all that. In my case, I am the architect and the builder. I love the way the edifice comes up, mapping itself to my imagined structure.'

'That sounds nice.'

'Isn't it? I am glad you feel the same way. For me, nothing is better than the final stage, which as you know is testing.'

'You test yourself?'

'Yes. I don't trust others. I try to crash my software, bring down what I have made. I throw everything at it. I will that it fails, that my bot dies before it is born. I become my worst enemy.'

'And when you can't?'

'That moment, when something I have made takes birth, it takes my breath away. I give it a name and I try to let go.'

He was breathless. When he raised his eyes, he saw her looking at him and the look in her eyes pleased him. He tried to give it a name.

'Now tell me about yourself,' she said.

He spoke in fits and starts. He wasn't interesting, he thought, after all his personal life was quite ordinary. But she listened to him with rapt attention. Over many cups of coffee, her attention never wavered. He began to like his own story.

'You are still a kattan,' said Leela.

To his surprise, he did not mind her calling him that.

'You are smiling,' said Leela. 'Just look at you!'

He stood in front of his mirror the next morning. 'I am in love,' he said.

Leela turned into an obsession. He tried to be in her vicinity, to catch her eye. He treasured the smile she parted with, now and then. He hovered around her for a month until her discomfort became obvious. She began avoiding the water cooler, the coffee machine and the canteen—places where they accidentally met.

He hated himself when he sneaked up one night into Leela's cubicle and hid a camera. He had her now, in his sights, through the day. A few days later, Leela bent back in her chair, unclasped her hair, gathered it and made a knot. And she looked into the camera lens, longer than was necessary. Asok jumped out of his chair, hot and bothered. Did she know? And yet?

That night he removed the camera. The next day he couldn't work. He left early, his mind awhirl. He fired his home machine, a powerful desktop, and he rustled up his pixies and elves. He had names for them, his cute little bots. Each was a compact software routine that he had coded with care. When they were ready to go, he hacked into Leela's laptop, her computers, her phone, her smartwatch and her exercise monitor. The bots marked their territory and stayed invisible. They acted as sensors, stalked her in every room, down every road. Under his guidance, they trolled her online persona, getting under her skin, understanding her better with each interaction.

Every night, Asok downloaded Leela's day. And he fed every bit of her into an algorithm. In a couple of months, he could say with surety that a version of Leela existed in the cloud and this Leela was his. He felt close to her, closer than ever before.

He introduced bots that began to affect her. She spent a lot of time online so he used random pings, push notifications, ads and reminders to unsettle her. She was made aware she was being 'watched'. It felt weird but she started looking under rugs, behind curtains and at the ceiling. Machines were closing in on her, she felt. In her sleep, she sensed worms feasting on her memory. Asok began appearing in her timelines, woven in by his insidious elves.

Asok hoped she would change, that she would view him differently, that at some point he would become what she was looking for.

The entire top management was there to receive the investors. The investors were from across the seas, from firms with names like Pacific and Atlantic. They had a following in their community. They had to be convinced. The CEO had briefed his team. 'The Corporation needs more money, a ton of it. We need to do something dramatic to convince these hard nuts.'

It began with a physical tour of the facility. The CTO led the walk.

'The landscape is Dell, not Apple,' he said. 'Black towers, black monitors, Windows and the odd Linux. The setting as you can see is geeky. Each is allowed a station that they can personalise.'

They stood at one, the inmate sat while the group looked around. Photographs of his partner, an infant, holiday snaps, to-do lists, some slogans. The group smiled and walked on.

'The central hall as you can see is a football field.'

On both sides were coffee machines, water dispensers and coolers. One side had windows that had tinted glass. There were no grilles. The view was of clouds and blue sky. The office was perched on the tenth floor.

'The language at lunch is a mix of English and Tamil,' said the CTO.

The key investor spoke up. 'Your salaries are high in comparison,' he said. 'Your monthly burn rate—who supports it?'

'Mezzanine investment,' said the CEO.

Looking out of the large bank of windows, the key investor said, 'Our view is long term. When I say long term, I mean ten plus years. But, and this is one of the many buts, I am a hands-on investor. If we put in money, I will be all over you.'

He had done his research. He knew the CTO of the company was a gaming addict, the CIO was on opioids and the CEO liked his drink. As the tour ended, the CEO bent at the waist and whispered into his ear.

'We have hacked into your company's database,' he said.

'What?'

'Our latest product, a beta called Vedic, has been installed in your servers.'

The chief investor's eyes bulged. 'The nerve. What the fuck will Vedic do?'

'We don't know,' said the CEO.

'Like hell!'

'But we have placed limits. No financial stuff, no legal chicanery.'

'I see. Then what will it do that is interesting to me?'

It was a good question.

'It will examine your portfolio companies and your potential investments, including us. It will recommend investment, divestments, exits and closures.'

The investor was surprised. 'The gall! You are trying to teach us? Through a piece of code?'

'A super bot, sir. Vedic has crunched data, corporate data of the last twenty years. It focuses on human failings.'

'Human failings?'

'Principally, attachment. Or what Vedic calls emotional inertia. All of us suffer from it. Secondly, illogic, especially in the face of changed circumstances. Lastly, the age-old curse of the investor—greed. It seems most investors suffer from these basic failings.'

'Are you trying to tell me how to do my job? Is this your way of impressing me?'

The CEO had gambled big time. Past the point of no return. 'Sir, we have allowed ourselves to be subject to this appraisal as well. I trust Vedic. I will respect its view on us.'

After a few minutes of examining Vedic's recommendations, the investor leaned back in his chair and smiled. 'You have balls,' he said.

'It is a win-win for us, sir,' said the CEO. 'We win either way. If Vedic screws us, then we stand vindicated. After all Vedic is what we are all about.'

'I see. Impressive,' said the investor. 'So, Vedic is already ready. Why do you need my money?'

'For our artificial intelligence project,' said the CEO and CIO in one voice.

Asok wasn't a team player. He switched off in group meetings, he rejected peer reviews and his emails were obnoxious. He endured in the Corporation because his moments of brilliance made up for everything else, including his poor work habits. He was working on the artificial intelligence project. He had attached sensors to cars to understand road rage, positioned them in department stores to study shopping patterns and hidden them in homes to record personal behaviour.

'People are being monitored by me,' he told Leela. 'They should be scared.'

'Why?'

'My bots know these people better than they know themselves. I know the small things they do, unnoticed. My algorithms can predict what these people are capable of.'

'How does that help?'

'The CIO says we can, as corporations, use this data, this understanding. We can target.'

Asok remembered a meeting when the CEO had asked, 'Could we actually end up manipulating people? Could we, at a tipping point, lead people over the edge?'

The CIO's reply was ingenuous. 'I don't know, sir. But I intend to find out.'

His budget presented a challenge. He needed to comb a million homes, invade privacy and collect reams of data.

'Exactly what will this achieve?' asked the CEO.

His explanation: 'Sir, data is our raw material. We need millions of gigabytes. Neural networks will comb this data and form associations and patterns. We will construct people in the cloud. Then our bots will arrive, not one or two, but an army. They will aim darts at these people and we will monitor their behaviour. More patterns and associations will emerge. Our cloud versions will keep improving and begin to resemble the people we are studying.'

The CIO had a dreamy look. 'The learning never stops,' he said, 'it is a relentless cycle. At some point, we will have a mirror reconstruction of each person we are studying. With sensors in place, we will descend from the cloud. You, sir, will be at the console. You will be what people call chance and coincidence.'

'Then it will be time to play dirty, sir,' said Asok's immediate boss.

'Time to play God, you nitwit!' said the CIO.

The Corporation had decided on a vertical. There were companies doing surveillance, some were improving sales through customer targeting. The Corporation chose interference. The mandate was to move machines from learning to empowerment.

'Sounds good,' said the CEO, stroking his chin. 'I have to ask the question. Is all of this legal?'

'Competition in Russia and the USA will kill us if we are slow,' said the CIO. 'They are ruthless exploiters of technology. They are neck-deep into interference. They are already manipulating elections, foisting presidents.'

'Let us go to work then,' said the CEO. 'We have the money.'

Months later, on Black Friday, while the First World shopped, Leela resigned. Her superiors scrambled to retain her and called her for lunch to make her a fresh offer. She was never seen again. By the time a breathless Asok arrived, she had vacated her apartment. His bots combed her virtual world but by then somebody had wiped her online presence clean.

Heads rolled in the Corporation. This was unacceptable. Leela was a critical resource working on a project that paralleled Asok's. Two teams were working independently on interference, a practice the Corporation found necessary. A search of her cubicle unearthed an A4 sheet. It had two words in Calibri font, evidence that she had a sense of humour.

Smoking Gun, it said.

Months elapsed, the artificial intelligence project took shape, and the mood in the Corporation was upbeat. On a given Sunday, a mosquito was Asok's companion for the night. It chose not to bite. It hovered in the vicinity of his ears and sang. The effect was of an enemy aircraft making sorties. The pitch got to him as did the relentlessness. He had a few ways of killing a mosquito. He tried. He clapped his hands in the dark and clutched his fist in vain. He sat up and contemplated his next move.

He left his room and walked out into the dark street. An oil lamp was burning under a tree. At the base of the tree, the roots had knotted. It was an old tree, and with leftover red, someone had painted a small gash on it one night. In no time, a temple had taken root. The deity was Kali, dark with a pink tongue.

He paused at the shrine and whispered a prayer. He thought he heard a noise. He felt uncomfortable. A rodent scurried past his legs. He returned feeling giddy.

The next morning, he sat before his home machines and blinked. He couldn't believe what he was seeing. While he was asleep, someone had sent him a starred message.

> Wake up Asok. Thank the lord for the sun. Take a deep breath of fresh air, be happy you are alive.
>
> Spare a thought now for your online persona. Somewhere in the bowels of a server farm, your engine is running. Your engine. It belongs to you, not Google, not Microsoft.
>
> Dear Asok, your engine is now ours.

Someone had hijacked his presence.

He developed a severe headache, his vision blurred. He stood unsteadily before his mirror, checked his skin where eruptions remained. He took one last look at the same old face. How could someone do this to him?

He showered, standing for a while under the steaming water. He emerged feeling better. He ran a comb through his hair. He took care to dress well. When he swiped his card and entered his quad, the rest of the team looked at him and their jaws dropped. He was well-dressed. Bold in his sartorial choices, yet for the first time, everything he wore came together very well.

He went directly to his boss's cabin and asked for an urgent meeting. Who should attend? 'Very senior people,' he said. The CEO showed up. The CTO and CIO were asked to attend.

'Coffee?' the CTO asked the room.

'I will have a cappuccino,' said Asok.

'You will what?'

'With demerara sugar please.'

His boss snorted. 'Can you even spell cappuccino? Till yesterday you were having Horlicks.'

'Doesn't matter,' said the CTO. 'Get him one. Now tell me what has happened?'

'Somebody is imitating me,' said Asok. 'Somebody very smart, very good.'

'Imitating?'

'This person has hacked into my online presence, used my ids unscrupulously and left no traces.'

The CEO looked relieved. 'You mean your social media accounts? That's just a password hack.'

'No, sir,' said Asok. 'This person took complete control of my bots.'

This was a code red breach. A disaster.

'You told us nobody could,' said the CTO.

Asok shrugged his bony shoulders.

'I thought my firewalls were ironclad. This somebody is out of the ordinary.'

'My question is why?' said the CEO. 'Why would someone do it?'

'They could have harmed us once they had control,' said the CTO. 'Did they?'

'No, sir.'

'Who could it be?'

'Could be a lone ranger,' said the CTO. 'These guys are so messed up, they do stuff like this for a lark, sometimes.'

'No, sir,' said Asok. 'Whoever did this has their own bots. Those bots took control of ours. Right now we are under the command of their machine. Their machine is learning even as we speak. I can feel it, sir, it is amongst us.'

Those in the room looked around. There was no visible change but every whisper of air felt eerie.

'This is not some chess game, damn it!' shouted the CEO. 'Who could it be? Foreign government? Cannot be India. Nobody out here is as skilled as we are.'

'Indian,' said Asok, sounding sure.

'How are you so sure?'

'The machine hacked into my playlist and left Tamil songs.'

The room was silent for a while. The seniors turned towards Asok, looked at him closely. They expected to see pride that had been punctured, an ego that had been waylaid. Asok looked calm. A little too calm.

'I am sure we can fight this,' said the CEO.

'Only if he allows us to,' said the CTO. 'He needs to cooperate. He is a hacker himself.'

'Can we not trace them, Asok?' asked the CEO. 'Just find out who it is and leave the rest to me.'

Asok shook his head. He had a look of admiration that he could no longer hide. 'Sir, their bots leave no trail. Their pixies and elves are shedding their garb like snakeskin. One of their bots lives and dies every nanosecond. It is mocking me.'

'What is this bot doing?' asked the CTO, looking a little scared.

'Sir,' said Asok, 'since yesterday, it has started changing my behaviour. I am helpless.'

He stood up holding his mug of cappuccino and his newfound dress sense was on display. He waved towards a ceiling corner where a camera and sensors were at work.

'What are you doing?' asked the CTO.

Asok was smiling, possessed, it seemed, by someone else.

'I have found myself,' he said. 'She has found me.' His voice sounded deeper, richer and more confident.

'She? Who is this she?' shouted his boss. 'Sit down first.'

'I have to leave, sir,' said Asok. 'It is time. I know it is her. I have to meet her. I have to introduce myself again.'

Phones began pinging, the room lights blinked and dimmed, the projector fan whirred and an image formed on the drop-down screen that had lowered itself. A song began playing through the office Alexa. A classic by Pink Floyd.

'What the hell is happening!' said the CEO.

The image coalesced on the screen. It was Leela, a pixelated stencil-cut version, and she spoke with a synthesised vocoder voice. 'Welcome,' she said.

Asok stood transfixed. Leela held out her arms.

'Welcome to the machine,' she said.

Long in the Tooth

Krishna Kumar used to be young. He stood forever at the door of his house in Alappuzha facing the backwaters. Behind him was the Arabian Sea. In Kerala, water is never far from your feet. Kumar has dark eyes; they search the horizon. A literacy percentage hangs proudly from a coconut tree. He is an inch taller than most. He likes the language of protest. He likes the flavour of the season called Left.

His state is verdant, it is the size of a communist country. It is famed for its plurality, its history, its ancient ports like Kollam and Calicut where Europeans beached. You can feel an undercurrent in its tea shops and colleges. Discussion runs around with its tail on fire and differences are deep-rooted. People hold their ground, they meet you halfway, like the local language does, a palindrome called Malayalam.

His mother is a matriarch. They have willed the land to her. She rules the household. She sits with her hair astray, rolling betel leaves, chewing the ears of her neighbours. Her legs bear bite marks of the dogs on the streets. She sniffs the acrid country arrack being swilled. Sickly sweet toddy is being tapped from trees. She spits. Small toads hop around her feet.

From a distance, she looks like a character from *The God of Small Things*, fashioned from grandmother stock. Close up, she looks like the poet Kamala Das, big and not all there. She was made to sit out her periods in the backyard, in 'unclean' isolation. She cursed her forbears and rend the men in her vicinity. A potted tulsi in the centre of the backyard withstood the barrage.

Kumar graduated with a bachelor's degree in fine arts from Thiruvananthapuram. The state was forever in ferment and Malayalees like him took up cudgels. Their deity was Che Guevara. His image was etched on walls, T-shirts and trees. The city of Alappuzha was full of career rebels. No system and no dispensation could satisfy them. The rebel badge gave their life meaning.

Artistic output? Its time would come.

He broke rank when he signed up for a postgraduate arts course in the faraway city of Baroda. He left early, while his family slept, and caught passenger trains that crawled up the West Coast, stopping at every station. He sat in the carriage doorway, dangling his legs, smoked weed and stared at the countryside. His beard grew, he felt forever young.

He arrived in Baroda in a haze, dragged his suitcase through two-wheelers and cows, and asked for directions from a stranger, a fellow student called Girish. Girish, an earnest wordsmith from Mumbai, came from a family that ran coaching classes for hapless students. They shared a chai at a tea shop and got talking. They ended up sharing a room in an apartment. Kumar remembered the date and the time. He remembered the few words they spoke. He did not remember his first class in the arts college. The glow of the long journey hadn't subsided and while he did last the first day, sitting erect, he was willing to swear that the retired doyen K.G. Subramanyan had handled the first lecture.

'Did the great KGS take our class today?' he asked Girish.

'My dear Malayalee, KGS retired from teaching while you were still a sperm.'

'Is it?' said Kumar, spitting out some tea leaves. 'By the way, I was a Nair sperm.'

'You are quite certain?'

'Yes. A Nair sperm is given to reflection.'

'Being the chosen one among millions of his co-workers?'

'Yes. A Nair sperm has questions. Like, why me, what is my existential purpose?'

'Of course. A respectable Malayalee question.'

They walked away towards the room they had rented.

'I can hear you thinking, comrade,' said Girish.

'They say that when I was born, I looked surprised,' said Krishna Kumar.

Their landlord was Mr Varadarajan. He had two spare rooms, one of which was occupied by Kumar and Girish, the other had Maya and Anjana. The men occupied the room facing east, the women chose to face the setting sun. A small corridor that divided the two rooms had a shelf for shoes and a chair to sit and wear them.

The four students came from middle India, from families that were careful with their fixed income. They knew how to wash their clothes and cook survival rations.

Maya set the tone for communal living. 'If the place looks like a dormitory, I will leave.'

She washed her hands constantly, swept the floor under the cupboards and pointedly wiped the toilet seat. She used cologne on herself and for good measure sprayed Kumar's vicinity.

'Mr Varadarajan is such a sweet fellow,' said Anjana.

He was a middle-aged bachelor who stayed by himself.

'Why?' asked Maya.

She was wary of such people.

'He looks harmless,' said Girish.

'Perhaps he is lurking for his moment,' said Maya.

It didn't help that Varadarajan told them, 'Anything you need, please come to me. Any time, day or night. Just knock on my door.'

Maya frowned. 'What did he mean?'

'The straighter a person is the hornier he sounds,' said Krishna Kumar.

'Unlike you,' said Anjana.

Through the half-open door to Varadarajan's room, they could see a desk, a television, a calendar and framed black-and-white photographs of his parents over which he had draped some wood roses.

Krishna Kumar slipped into his room every now and then. They became drinking buddies. They wore sleeveless vests and terry towels, and drank rum in small glass tumblers. Late into the night, they scratched mosquito bites and argued about Tamil culture, Malayalam films and the long-term benefits of trekking to the holy shrine of Sabarimala.

Maya would overhear and worry whenever the volume rose. She would pace her room while Girish and Anjana watched, each plugged into music. Girish liked jazz and alternate rock, Anjana liked Hindi film music from an era when actors made eyes at each other, kissed behind flowers and rolled in the hay.

'Are you two in love?' asked Maya. She felt threatened.

True to form, Krishna Kumar had political ambitions. The campus was an arena rife with possibilities. He imagined himself as a student leader in their senior year. He wanted his flatmates on his team.

'You have the arrogance,' said Anjana.

'And the required scruffiness,' said Maya.

'But you lack the credentials.'

'Why, who is good enough to be your hero?'

Anjana had high standards. In her pantheon were Walter Benjamin, Borges, Andrei Tarkovsky and Louise Bourgeois. Krishna Kumar wasn't going to fill in for them in a hurry.

'And who is your hero, madam?' Kumar asked Maya.

'My hero has a bath every day,' she said.

Girish thought himself a dude; after all, he was from Mumbai. He often gawked at Kumar, taken up by his quaintness and rusticity, and his rapacious need to prove himself. Kumar was a subject who could help hone his skills as a writer.

'I will support you,' he said. 'We will have banners, slogans and rallies. The student election could be our outreach project.'

The election project was a failure. A few months elapsed; time hung heavy on campus. Kumar cut a forlorn figure. He was visibly restless. He tried spending time in the library, he leafed through books looking for inspiration. Discourse in the art world was dense, the language was academic. His English comprehension was severely tested.

'I can't,' he said.

'Can't what?'

'I cannot paint like you, Maya.'

'Even your drawing is terrible,' she said.

Kumar's line was an uncertain one, it was a rat in the dark that had sniffed a cat in the air and was seeking an escape route.

'I lack fluency. I don't know where to begin. I keep over-painting.'

'You are in luck,' said Anjana. 'Contemporary art is more than just drawing and painting. You can be poor in both and get away.'

'I can carve,' said Krishna Kumar.

'Really? What will you carve? Stone?'

'No. I meant air. I can perform. That is what I am meant to be, a performer.'

He began missing classes and spent more and more time in his room smoking up a storm. This had happened before. Students who were unable to stay the course had gradually dropped out.

Anjana disliked him and his gaze, directed as it was at her breasts. She never said anything harsh to him—someday she would. Her manner was intelligent. She spoke of him in the third person in his presence.

'A man who never paused, who never watched a garden grow, what will he take away from this world?'

'Nothing?' said Girish.

'Yes, nothing.'

'Are you talking about me?' asked Kumar.

'Yes. There is something futile about you, Krishna Kumar,' she said. 'You think you are meant for bigger things and a larger life than a mere artist's existence.'

'I am the resistance,' said Kumar.

His motive force set Girish on edge. His nervous energy was fearsome.

Smoking came naturally to Kumar. He ran through two packs of twenty every day; each cigarette lit another. His bed had poor posture, it sagged in the middle; his pillow was permanently propped. The wall that faced him had a poster from the Cuban revolution and a still from the film *The Year of Living Dangerously*.

'One half of my room belongs to Kumar,' said Girish. 'I have to hold him at bay.'

The morning sun traversed past them to the corridor outside. The room opposite welcomed the setting sun. Maya and Anjana liked evenings when the light was mellow, light that looked like the tea they sipped, sitting in their rattan chairs, legs gathered below them.

'So, you are friends now?'

'Yes. For life.'

Kumar did not complete the course requirements. He was glad when the academic year came to an end. His grades were terrible, his teachers were frustrated by his lack of application.

'Go back to Thiruvananthapuram and take a gap year,' said one of his teachers.

He left for his home state the way he came, catching trains in sequence.

'What will I tell my family?'

The further south he went, the more uncertain was his journey. He was tempted to get off somewhere in the middle, in a strange town where he could lose himself for a while. He called Girish from a remote station.

'Baroda taught me nothing!'

'Nobody can teach you anything, comrade.'

Within hours of arriving in Alappuzha, Kumar was missing his three friends in Baroda. He wanted to meet them again but had no wish to return and complete the course. Days passed by, weeks added up and he stayed on in Kerala.

Girish called. 'Where are you? College just opened.'

Kumar was incoherent.

'I am not well.'

'Call me back when you are well. Will you?'

He did not. But a few months later, he wrote them letters by hand, stamped the covers and dropped them into the red postbox near his house.

Dear Maya, Anjana and Girish,
Here I am in Alappuzha, a little older, facing a situation. Every situation in Kerala is a self-goal. The past collides with the future and the present remains less than satisfactory.

'Where do you think you are going?' my family asked me.

I have no role to play in my large and extended family. I do not fit into any slot. When I was away at art school, nobody missed me.

'You have returned suddenly,' said my father.

My brothers and sisters gathered one evening. My uncles and aunts also came. They took a close look at me. I could see they were checking boxes, like potential groom, possible breadwinner, God forbid, a black sheep.

I have joined hands with my maternal uncle. He lives on a houseboat, a kettuvallom, which he plies on the backwaters. It is a large boat with two bedrooms for hire. We have an arrangement with resorts and we host their guests for a night or two. The backwaters are calm, the boat is slow; life on it is meant to be leisurely. The afternoons are so drowsy. Sweat forms slowly, each drop takes ages to fall.

I am the handyman on this kettuvallom. My uncle calls himself captain. Captain is a gifted cook, a nadan chef who uses local spices and coconut oil, cooks in an earthen pot called mannchatty, and produces chicken curry, prawn curry and beef fry. The oil and spice tickle the taste buds and set fire to the tongue. Customers have tears in their eyes, yet they ask for more.

The mannchatty is coated with sticky grease. I have to clean the damn chatty every day and I have to clear the bones.

My family thinks I have changed. One year in Baroda, they say, has made me thoughtful. It seems I walk now with my head slightly bowed. My father is a writer and he says my fearless son has withdrawn into a private fable; he looks like he is carrying his thoughts around like precious cargo. He says only a young traditional girl can break this spell.

Your friend,

Kumar

Nobody replied to his letter. He went to the post office and kept asking. He sat inside and wrote another letter.

Dear Maya, Anjana and Girish,

I miss the excitement of Baroda. House boating is becoming predictable. Yesterday, a well-endowed European found a large spider on her towel while bathing. She ran out topless. Other than that, there is nothing to report. I wash the towels and bedsheets and I know people find boat rides stimulating. I believe when you make out in a car it creaks. When you make love on a kettuvallom, the water ripples.

I am counting ripples and the days that are going by.

Today I was alone and it was a moonless night. The light came from a traditional oil lamp. I stood still on my boat on the bow. My stance was precarious. I wanted to dance and I did. Only my eyebrows were alive and they were trying to express like the great Mohanlal did in the film *Vanaprastham*. The principal character in *Vanaprastham* is a low-caste, male, Kathakali dancer. Mohanlal received many accolades for his portrayal, for his grasp of the Kathakali dance form.

Friends, I was Mohanlal tonight. I was Kunhikuttan in *Vanaprastham* and I performed on my kettuvallom as a tribute. The boat swayed with my weight but the water rippled only when I moved my eyes. In Kathakali, the eyes speak and percussion listens, and then the two tango and flirt for a while.

Kathakali dancers are actors as well. Their faces are painted in layers. They wear bright frocks and an elaborate headdress. They look like oversized dolls. The music is percussion, the rhythms are spare and the gestures are minimal.

I am a student of this dance form at this timeless place called Kalamandalam in Kerala, the true home of Kathakali. Every performance I have seen here has rendered me mute.

Love,
Krishna

A few weeks passed and then another letter appeared in Baroda. The ink Krishna had used changed from para to para.

Dear Maya, Anjana and Girish,

I can only write about today. Today I read the local language newspaper. They write about a different world. Things do happen around here in Alappuzha. It seems a dog died while walking. A line of patients recovered by hugging a Mayi. Elsewhere a Malayalee aunty, who hardly spoke two words of Sanskrit, began to recite the Upanishads verbatim.

On every page, there is politics. Thankfully. I still believe in resistance, like in the old days. My father hates it. He says I see a yoke on my shoulder even if I haven't spent an honest day on a farm.

There are hordes of tourists who come to Kerala every day. I get no rest from politeness and good service. Now I have to do the dishes. Another month of this and I will kill somebody nearby.

What is happening to my life?

The family is trying to fix my alliance. It is time to leave. Otherwise, I will settle down with Kutty Selvi, a young damsel in potential distress. I will ruin her world.

I will come back soon to Baroda. Please call me, please tell me you are still there.

Love,

Krishna

Within a couple of days, another letter arrived in Baroda.

Dear friends,

I had a late-night session with my uncle. He is a good storyteller. We drank some local brew we call kashayam and once we were high, I showed him what I painted in Baroda. He stroked his beard. Times have changed, he said.

'Are they any good?' I asked.

He said, look at the night sky. I looked. 'Do you see the full moon?'

'It is shining,' I said.

'Maybe,' he replied. 'But the light does not belong to the moon. Do you understand?'

I did not.

'Show me other artists,' he said.

The pictures he liked from what I showed him were painted by the artist Surendran Nair. He saw them again and again. He told me, 'When you dance, you copy the great Mohanlal. When you paint, you are copying this Nair.'

That hurt me. 'You are an old bandicoot,' I told him. 'One day the backwaters will flood, and hopefully, you will die of drowning.'

Your lost friend,
Krishna

Krishna Kumar slept fitfully, he dreamt, he visualised an ignoble end, sliding down the roof tiles of his house, grabbing at protrusions, tipping over the edge and landing on his head on the concrete below.

He woke up, took a deep breath, leaned as far as his outstretched arm could go and a glass tumbler toppled and shattered on the floor. He waited for someone to show up. Nobody did.

Things needed to happen for Kumar. He was drowning in the still waters of Alappuzha.

He sneaked into the railway station and bought a one-way ticket to Baroda. Two years had passed since his return. Twenty-four months.

In the train, Kumar tossed and turned and dreamt of Mohanlal. Mohanlal was dressed like him, he essayed the role of his life. He played the role of a man who could not countenance his fate, who couldn't summon the energy to fight it.

Within minutes of his arrival in Baroda, Krishna Kumar was back on the campus in a seminar room. A heated discussion was taking place. The title was grandiose—Seminal Texts in Indian Art

Important art historians had singled out three texts deserving the title of seminal. Girish was there, vigorously opposing the choices. He was by now a respected senior, gaining a reputation. He was an ideal academic, one the faculty liked; given a chance they would have adopted him for safekeeping. It was a time when the only seminal activity happening on campus was in mixed dorms.

'Welcome back, comrade,' said Girish.

'Look at you!' said Kumar. 'You are not half the rebel you used to be.'

'I am now part of the establishment.'

They looked hard at each other, holding back other things they wanted to say and do. They both realised how much they had missed being together. They left for their familiar tea shop for a glass of chai.

'Everything has changed,' said Girish.

'Maya?'

'She has moved to Mumbai. Two years from now, she will unveil her first solo show.'

'Anjana?'

'She has moved to Delhi.'

'I hope you will be staying on?'

Girish shrugged. 'There isn't much to do here. I have tried the academic option. It is exciting but it doesn't pay very well.'

'So?'

'I might move to Mumbai as well. I have a job offer from a newspaper.'

Kumar realised that he had returned late and was likely to be alone in Baroda.

'What kept you in Alappuzha?' asked Girish.

'I don't know,' said Kumar. 'I was confused. I still am.'

'Did you learn anything?'

'Kathakali,' said Kumar. 'I tried. In Kalamandalam, the best school.'

'Did you qualify?'

'No. It is still a work in progress.'

'And why have you returned?'

'I don't know,' said Kumar.

Nobody described the summer when the days were long and the dust never settled, but when the monsoon came to Baroda, people described it and they called it rain, and when the rain entered their homes, they called it water, and when it poured and poured and the river woke up, spread and turned on its side, they called it a flood.

Krishna Kumar was born in a place where nobody described the rain. It came every year in May and left in September. It was a family member more than a guest, a provider of freshwater that drove back the sea for a while. For the people who lived on the backwaters, it was a way of life.

Kumar was born in Kuttipuram, which means a small place, and it is a bloody small place, but it is like Baroda in one small way, a river runs through it. The Bharatapuzha runs through Kuttipuram, and when the rains are hard, it swells just like the Vishwamitri does in Baroda.

Floods are a bad time for artists and revolution, but the rain doesn't know it.

The year Kumar returned to Baroda, it rained again without letting up. It was a bad time for the young man from Kerala. He stood alone, far from his home state. Water lapped his feet. The phone rang, he waited. It kept ringing. He removed the device carefully from his pocket and answered. It was Maya.

'Thanks for calling back,' he said. He was close to tears. He spoke to her about this and that, about failure, about stepping stones to nowhere. Maya listened patiently.

'You are beginning to remind me of men who grow old, turn bitter and die young,' she said.

Kumar looked at the phone in his hand. He dropped it into a puddle of water. He walked to the railway station and forced his way into an unreserved compartment. When the train reached its destination, he caught another. He arrived in Kerala a week later with lice in his hair, dirt in his fingernails and blood in his spit.

His family rallied behind him, they gave him a room with a window, his mother bought canvas and paint, a few brushes. He spent time in the room, he sat before an easel, from time to time, he sketched in a notebook. He did paint a few works and showed them to his mother. She was sweet, she smiled, happy that he was occupied. When he saw the works after a gap of a month, he was depressed. Something was missing. He had no idea what it was, but that something was always missing.

He remembered being frustrated as a student in Baroda and Anjana had tried to teach him patience. 'Art is a gradual unravelling,' she had said. Girish had been more forceful. 'Why are you obsessed with artistry? There are other things.'

He stacked the canvases below the window, facing the wall. Sooner or later, it would rain and the water would pour in. He was beyond caring.

'Travel,' said his mother. 'Go away for a few days, it will help you.'

He went to the railway station and caught a train, then another. He did this for two weeks, sleeping on trains, subsisting on platform food and facilities. On his return leg, he visited the art Biennale in the nearby city of Kochi. His face was mottled, his hair was matted. He looked like a free-range country chicken, aged, full of protein but too ugly for the knife. He spent three days wandering through the sites and installations in the Fort Kochi area. There was poetry written in series all over the city, multi-channel videos that filled rooms, sculpture and site-specific installations. A few paintings as well. The weather was uncomfortable, warm and muggy. He wore himself out for three days looping around the various sites, and in the evenings, he drank himself into a stupor.

He couldn't leave the place. He found himself returning to a particular work. It was by the well-known artist Atul Dodiya. It was a life-size work, it had what looked like a usable noose made of thick rope that hung from an upright scaffolding. Next to it was a stretched canvas on which the artist had drawn a poem. The work scared him.

On his third visit, he gathered the courage to get close to the work. It was macabre, he felt, the noose looked ready for use; the scaffolding would easily bear his weight. It was a performance piece, he thought. All it needed was him and a stool.

He read the poem painted on the canvas. The poem was by Allama Prabhu, a twelfth-century mystic poet from the Kannada region. The poem spoke of a wilderness in the sky, about a hunter in that wilderness holding a deer in his hands. He read the last few lines aloud.

The hunter will not die
till the beast
is killed.
Awareness is not easy,
is it,
O Lord of the Caves?

For some reason he could not fathom, he was profoundly moved. He sat before the installation, his legs folded under him, and he wept like a child.

K.P. Krishnakumar was born in Kuttipuram, Kerala in the year 1958. He earned a diploma from the School of Arts in Trivandrum. He received a post-diploma from Santiniketan, West Bengal. He was part of the Indian Radical Painters' and Sculptors' Association, a group that had a militant agenda and wished to radically interrogate Indian art of the time.

As an artist, he had his first solo show in 1975. He also participated in group shows.

On 26 December 1989, Krishnakumar, aged 31, woke up, sipped tea, shaved his stubble and took a wash before dressing up. He then made a rope from thin twines, slung it from a wooden ceiling and hanged himself.

No satisfactory reason has been ascribed to his suicide.

His mother, Ammallukutty Amma, stays in the Palakkad district of Kerala, surrounded it seems by her son's unsold paintings.

This is not his story.

Acid

It was an old bungalow in the dockyard area, ground-plus-one on a small plinth with only elbow room around it. At the rear, there was a Hercules cycle that had gathered rust, on the side a motorbike, a forgotten model called Yezdi. Its tires were worn, its fenders had dented and its brake light had shattered. They walked in like they owned the place. They shouldered the door and the latch broke. It swung open and listed. Dust rose from the floor and the head constable sneezed. They looked around, not expecting trouble, anything for that matter. The wall paint looked flaky; the windows had cobwebs. In the corners, there were roaches.

They found him in the last room, a small one. He was sleeping on a cot, a metal contraption that had a colourful checked rug on it—a jamakkalam. He was wearing shorts and nothing else.

'Should we take anything with us, other than this rowdy?'

'What is the smell; it smells, this place, like an open toilet. Hey, come here, stand still. Look up. When did you bathe?'

They checked the tap in the corner latrine. No water. There was cardboard over the commode and a few flies buzzed around the cracked window.

'Just get the hell out, quickly. Put everything in a bag. Move, come on, move.'

Why was there no one else in the house? A question they would address later. The vagrant in their grasp did not look like a tenant, leave alone a homeowner.

'Dai, porki!'

He came to, opened his eyes, and gagged. They dropped him near the gate. He fell to the ground and retched. Nothing came out. His insides were empty, what he had was bile, acid from an empty stomach. The rough handling did not affect him, not one bit. They tore his collar, a couple of buttons flew, and when they dragged him his footwear shredded. In the jeep, he flopped onto the bag that held his belongings. The jeep rattled, the wheels thudded over potholes, and he went to sleep.

'He doesn't look like the criminal you are looking for,' said the head constable.

Inspector Murthy had his doubts. He didn't show them.

The boy died. It remained an anonymous death. In the mortuary, nobody came to claim him. He was cremated and his ashes strewn in an empty plot nearby. Much later, his relatives showed up and created a racket, so a team was asked to investigate. They were reluctant and they were haphazard. They said the boy did not exist in the dockyard station files. The register, a big one with handwritten entries, had no mention of the custody of a young man on the said date. There was no record of a custodial interrogation, no transcript of any sort.

Attendance on that day was normal. Besides Inspector Murthy, there was a head constable and two of his minions, all of whom had signed the register of attendance. In the outer office, there was a clerk and a peon. An ayah came in twice every day to clean the place. She wasn't on the rolls.

They couldn't do without her. She dusted the place, swabbed every surface and cleaned the toilets. On certain days, she was sent into the room at the rear to clean up after interrogations. If there was a witness to the aftermath, it was her. Luckily, or perhaps by design, she was a mute. She couldn't speak. Fit for purpose, according to those who knew Inspector Murthy.

Anybody else in this station, the investigating team asked.

'Muruga,' said Murthy, looking up and folding his hands. 'Only Lord Muruga.'

Fit for purpose. Muruga was a deity that would never speak.

After the incident, Murthy was reassigned to the Kotturpuram Police Station. He couldn't stand the place. He couldn't stand boredom. His new assignment was in a part of the city that crime did not favour. Some stations were hives for thieves; they were situated in colonies that were havens for petty larceny. On an average day, they resembled a railway station, or a busy thoroughfare, with people sitting on whatever was available, groups standing in corners, complainants pressing over each other at the register, and in the lock-up, usually at the rear, would be a motley bunch of regulars who came and went depending on how tired the cops felt. The Kotturpuram station was dull beyond measure. Minutes crawled with the slow deliberation of a cow with a full belly. Murthy stayed sane by picking his teeth, wandering to the tea stall next door and reading the Tamil newspapers, listening to the tirades of people waiting at the bus stop. He could sense the impatience of the average citizen. He called it the frustration of the incompetent. He wanted to line up the complainers and beat them up.

'You know who lives in this locality? People with modest means. Educated people. Brought up by parents, two to a home, married till they died, usually a few days apart. And they work for a living, mostly to bring up children. It is a cycle that was invented here. This is middle-class Kotturpuram colony life. They are all somberis. Pedigree dogs with orderly bowels. Hopeless fellows.'

'Sir, is it true?' asked the local head constable.

'What?'

'That when you were in the dockyard station one somberi died?'

'So?'

'Teeth were missing, sir. And some fingernails.'

'Who told you?'

The constable smiled. 'Everybody knows about you, sir. We all know why you are here in this peaceful place.'

The day the crimes started to happen, Inspector Murthy looked to the heavens and said 'Muruga', with some feeling. A rash of burglaries that were committed, it seemed, by an intelligent person. So much was strange about these robberies. The victims were old couples, mostly brahmins. The larceny happened in the dead of night in almost complete darkness. The fuse box would be tampered with, the current switched off. If the occupants woke up, they would be tied up and spoken to firmly, and if they attempted to shout, they would be threatened. Most victims claimed they were half-asleep, dreaming, and could not remember what the thief looked like. Medium height, that much they were certain. His face was covered—he wore some kind of scarf. And one more thing. He sounded apologetic.

The thief spoke in English. His grammar was faultless and he insisted on conversing with them on any topic they wished to. He was never in a hurry to leave.

Murthy was impressed with this thief. At one crime scene, the rascal showed an acute awareness of the circuitry of a burglar alarm. At another, he had cooked himself a meal and then spent more than an hour regaling his victims with drunken poetry. He was a chatty fellow with an engaging manner. What he took away was what he could find in the modest homes that he chose to raid. Very little. It was odd that he chose such houses and neighbourhoods.

An elderly brahmin, a victim, actually pleaded with Murthy. 'If you ever catch him, don't be cruel.'

'This fellow is a madayan,' said the head constable. 'A certified dolt.'

There were so many affluent homes with rich pickings that he had ignored. Why? A burglary had to have a larger purpose. It was not meant to be reduced to a social outing.

'He is mocking us,' said Murthy. 'He is mocking the police.'

In public, Murthy exhibited good manners and a facility for language. He was educated all the way up to a graduate degree. He could spell coriander and he could recite a rhyme in his sleep. At official functions, his behaviour was deliberate and polished, as if he was aware that people, particularly his teachers, were still watching.

There was a chink in his make-up, and it had to do with pain, specifically its threshold. There were, on his arms, some self-inflicted marks, the kind that hurt but did not threaten life. They were attempts on his part to understand pain and the power of its anticipation. Pain had a special place in his make-up. He liked the fact that it always won. There was a point in every interrogation when it became unbearable and it was pleasing to watch when that happened. 'Muruga,' he would say, at that moment. 'Lord have mercy.'

Inspector Murthy looked at his vibrating phone. It was an unknown number. He always answered, he felt as a policeman he had to.

'Murthy,' he said.

'Inspector?'

The voice was low, he imagined a soft-spoken person, short perhaps.

'Yes, this is Inspector Murthy.'

'I need to meet you,' said the voice, now sounding a little urgent. Man with a beard, thought Murthy. Possibly a limp or some form of deformity.

'Why? And who is calling?'

'Sir, I cannot say just now. Please don't hang up.'

Murthy had a pin in his hand. His legs were crossed on his table, his shoes pointing to the fan that was whirring at maximum speed. He picked his teeth and waited.

'Sir, this has to do with the burglaries.'

The inspector sat up. He pulled a pad towards him and took out his pen.

'I am listening,' he said.

'I will talk when I meet you,' said the voice. 'Tell me when I can come.'

'You will come to the station?'

'Yes, sir. One request.'

Later, when Murthy called the head constable, he tried to remember the exact words that man had spoken. Darkness. He wanted to meet Murthy in total darkness. He wanted to meet him in his pickle chamber. He knew there was one at the rear of the station where Murthy conducted his questioning, and he possibly knew much more. Yet he was willing to submit himself to that chamber.

'Clean up the place, use antiseptic and open the windows. Place one chair in the corner, then shut everything and draw the blinds. He will come directly into the room from the side entrance.'

At ten that night when the station was quiet, Murthy heard the side door open. A short figure entered the dark room and he could barely discern his outline as he walked to the chair and sat. He could hear him breathing.

'Your name?'

'Sir, later. Please.'

'Okay. I am not happy with all this but let us continue. Tell me, I am here.'

'Sir,' said the man. 'I conducted the burglaries. It was me.'

'What?' said the head constable. He should not have spoken. He wasn't supposed to be there.

'Leave the room!' said Murthy. His junior let himself out.

The conversation continued for twenty minutes. The head constable stood outside the door and strained his ears but all he heard was a low monologue, punctuated by some short questions. He was called in and asked to turn on the light. The man had left.

'You let him go?'

Murthy nodded. There was a table in front of him that had the tools of his trade. A pair of pliers, a packet of cigarettes and a matchbox.

'He is the burglar. I did not see him, I don't know his name and I don't know where he stays.'

The head constable scratched his head.

'Sir?

'He steals in total darkness. You want to know why?'

'Sir?'

'He steals because he cannot get a job. You want to know why?'

Murthy knocked his head with his fist, a sign of frustration. For once he wasn't sure what he should be doing. He came from the school of summary justice and here was a man who had confessed voluntarily and he had let him go.

'Why, sir?'

'I will tell you. The bloody fellow is an acid victim,' said Murthy. 'Two years ago, he got married, a love marriage, and his wife's family chased him and threw a bottle of acid in his direction. They ended up maiming him. He lost his face; it just… melted.'

Murthy tried to imagine what he looked like. He had seen an acid victim and the image of that woman still haunted him. 'You know what he told me?'

'Sir?'

'I wish I had lost my eyesight. That's what he said.'

The head constable tut-tutted, shifting from one foot to the other. 'Poor fellow,' he murmured.

Inspector Murthy had slipped into a reverie. He looked distracted and confused.

'A year ago, his wife left him.'

'Should we close the case?' asked the head constable. 'Sir, did he say he would stop his thieving?'

Murthy smiled, remembering the young fellow's parting shot. 'He told me the burglaries will continue.'

The constable swallowed, then took the plunge. 'And you let him go, Inspector Murthy?'

There was reproach in his voice. In his mind was something bordering on a reprimand.

Murthy was expecting this response. The ayah, who had been called for the usual post-interrogation clean-up, entered at the time and started sweeping the room. 'What should I do?' asked Murthy. She continued sweeping, her head bowed, the end of her saree tucked between her teeth. Murthy looked into a corner where shadows were playing tricks.

'Muruga?' he said.

Old Vine Zinfandel

My mother said, 'I am feeling old.'

I rose from my chair.

'Where are you going?'

'Nowhere.'

It was the right word for the place she was in—my plight in the bargain.

I wandered to the window, she followed me with her eyes. Her face was all that was visible, she was hidden beneath a large pink comforter, a soft, formless marshmallow.

'The last time you just disappeared.'

Her eyes were swollen, her mouth distended.

'You just woke up?'

She yawned, her breath stank.

'What time is it?'

'Does it matter?'

'That's the worst thing to tell someone.'

I hated that she yawned through the day, that she lay in bed. This is a hospice, I kept reminding her, not a hospital.

'You are not a patient!'

'What am I then?'

'You are a… a guest.'

'No, that doesn't sound right,' she said. She sniffled. 'I am an inmate.'

She had an adjustable bed with levers and side rails. I turned the lever and raised her back.

'Hungry?'

'I am never hungry here. I miss that feeling.'

Three meals came by the clock, measured portions in neat trays. Attendants spooned the soup, speared morsels and wiped her spittle.

She began laughing.

'What?'

'Nothing,' she said.

The place was clean, despite everything. The city of Chennai fought a running battle against flies, mosquitos, roaches and rodents. They loved human waste, there was plenty at the home she was in.

'Do you know they bathe me? Do you have any idea how embarrassing that is?'

'No.'

She sniffled again. 'I am no longer proud of my body.'

'Why don't you walk outside?' I said. 'Why don't you...?'

'Twice a day male attendants wheel me out, for fresh air and vitamin D.'

This was what the brochures had promised. Assisted living. They had also promised there would be no palliative care cases. Those were mental, especially the cancer patients who raged mostly against the dying light.

'You brought the Dictaphone?'

I placed the gadget between us.

'Don't record everything.'

She made me erase her moaning. I switched it on and waited.

'I feel so useless,' she said. 'I am defenceless. Attendants enter at will, poke needles into me while I sleep. They speak about me to each other in my presence. I deserve better.'

'You do,' I said.

She was without make-up, her hair uncombed, her nightgown climbing her hairy legs.

'I do?'

This was the best Odissi dancer the country had seen. She had a stage presence in her prime, she was a prima donna backstage who took an hour to wear a full set of jewellery, a heavy silk saree and fresh flowers in her hair. A make-up assistant highlighted her piercing eyes. Another made sure everything was tucked in and secured. Then she stepped onto the stage, applause greeted her in waves. People rose, cameras flashed, her feet moved, the earth caved.

'I have been dreaming lately.'

'Mother,' I said, 'you sleep early, you wake up late.'

'Last night your father showed up, the one you haven't met.'

I said nothing.

'When did you come?'

'What do you care?'

My visits were regular. Despite everything I came. I was at an age when retirement beckoned, a scary thought. I had no steady source of income. The visit to the home was an imposition. The inmates were old and infirm, some were invalid. The staff was overly cheerful. Everything was white and bright, there were paintings on the wall, the curtains were colourful. If you stayed long, like I did, you noticed other things: IV lines, bags gathering fluids, adult nappies hanging heavy, pans below beds and, in the dust bins, some red-brown swabs. There was a smell that clung to me when I left the place.

The home was in a distant suburb, a few kilometres off the national highway, three buildings amidst vast, empty fields. Two mud tracks led up to them. Near the entrance gate, between a temple and a church, were ambulances. There was a housing section, a meals hall and a modest kitchen. There was an activity centre with indoor games and a television. There were more wheelchairs in the place than chairs.

'You met the Ayurveda doctor?'

I had gone to a house without a board where a doctor without a certificate gave me dark potions that smelt from a distance.

'My joints are so stiff. I am having trouble with buttons. Since yesterday, there is a twitch in my left leg.'

'The doctor said don't eat onions and garlic. And eat less lentils. Are you listening?'

She pointed to the gap beneath the door, to cracks in the wall where the newly formed stonework had crumbled. There were lizards getting into her room.

'There is a big one. Can you see him?'

When she slept, she dreamt she was an insect, smaller than a priest's toe. She couldn't fly.

'He will get me,' she said.

The lizard moved slowly in her direction. His eyes rotated, his tongue forked. My mother shivered.

'Amma,' I said, 'what have you become?'

A dancer who could twirl on her toes, tall, statuesque, born to grace the stage, to impale her adoring fans with her large, expressive eyes.

'When I struck a pose, I would pause and turn into a deity. The stage became a temple.'

I was tasked to write about her. The project was hampered by the games she played.

'Do you know who your father is?'

This was a taunt more than a question. There were many men in her life according to sources, sources that took vicarious pleasure in guessing what went on in her storied life. She married more than once. Temple weddings, she said.

Which temples?

'How does it matter?'

The first was an old man, feeble, a father figure who belonged to the 1950s in a town called Karaikudi. He was a Chettiar from a prosperous business family, he had a mansion the size of a fort. Ten steps up from the road was the entrance, a huge carved teakwood door.

I spent summers in that mansion till a family fight erupted, relatives surfaced and they usurped the place. Amma landed in Chennai where my elder brother Ravi and I stayed in her family house under the care of a maternal uncle.

Money came in driblets, from performances, from certain donors. We went to a convent school. I wore hand-me-downs, sizes awry, some loose threads and half-broken buttons. My brother was a star and I was moon shadow.

Amma started a school where she tried to teach Odissi. The dance school was one of many in Adyar. The school made for a noisy home. We didn't mind. For a while, girls came home, each more beautiful than the other.

'Chettiar loved me,' said Amma. 'He had a piercing gaze, and he knew his music. I would lie in his vicinity and he would keep looking at me. He liked feeling my pulse. It has a different timbre, he would say.'

Her eyes misted over.

'He attended my performances, sat on the side, dreamy, like he had inhaled something. After an hour, he couldn't sit and they would take him away.'

'And he called you…'

'By my name. Kamala.' She said it like he did, with a degree of affection.

Now Kamala was old. Most mornings she was fine. Then the day caught up with her.

'What exactly is wrong with you?'

She had a harsh, dry cough, poor digestion and frequent headaches.

'Some kind of allergy,' the doctor had said.

In the hunt for an allergen, she gave up many things. A pared-down life made things worse. Stop complaining, we told her.

'You boys don't listen.'

Ravi and I were in our fifties, an age when we had our own stash of grouses. I stayed in Chennai, Ravi was in Dubai. He was impatient and dismissive. She spoke to me. 'Ravi doesn't understand. I don't want people telling me, you are old, so does it really matter? What is inside you has let you live for so long, so why hunt it down?'

'Amma, there was a time when all that bothered you were your tired feet.'

Ravi set his glass down, it held nouveau Beaujolais, a light red wine that he bought on impulse from a supermarket, a cavernous place that sold things by the bushel. Ravi was single, by choice. Most days he was alone. He was number three in the pecking order, the CEO was a polished Brit, the COO was an Arab, an absentee landlord.

Ravi designed the systems and made himself redundant. This gave him time to pursue his interests. He took his holidays seriously. He was afraid of returning to India. India from a distance assumed a fearful form, every day a disaster, every other day a strange mishap. His friends in Chennai complained when he called, his mother stoked his guilt, Kumara, his brother, kept asking for money.

He stayed in a compound that had thirty villas, two swimming pools, a vast clubhouse and hedges trimmed to perfection. Abundant help that came from all corners of Asia cleaned, cooked and handled the appliances. Two refrigerators stood like sentries in an open kitchen. In between was a wine chiller that held five continents.

Shopping was fun, a sport, a pastime. He drove a large American SUV, marvelling at the roads, the large malls, the multilevel parking. He dragged a large trolley past carrel after carrel, picking, choosing, replacing. There was so much he didn't need. He wished Amma would visit him, his brother Kumara too, and both could then see what they were missing.

He liked the Gulf landscape. No politicians, journalists who did not dig deep, glossy newspapers that packaged the banal. Vertical glass towers, water in public spaces in large concrete saucers. Plants and lawns on a drip feed. A few dust storms, a large airport straining to cope. He wandered through bakeries sniffing bread, he paused at rotisseries where knives sliced through shawarma, meat was impaled on skewers and vegetables were stewed in vinegar.

He was part of a group of oenophiles, serious fellows who swirled, sniffed, sipped and spat into buckets. They were European, unused to an Indian with knowledge of wine. Ravi had a developed nose that could sift through spices.

'I heard Dubai has ghettos,' said Kumara. 'I read the labour class is put up there.'

'I stay in a high-class ghetto,' Ravi said. 'We love it here, the comfort, the convenience and the security.'

A few years of stasis followed. Ravi overstayed. 'You are no longer at the forefront of your profession,' warned one of his friends. 'More exciting things are happening in India.'

She coughed, it sounded hoarse. Inside her throat was an irritable pincer.

'No phlegm,' she said.

The doctor peered, adjusting his face mask. The torchlight travelled inside her looking for telltale signs. He straightened and searched for his stethoscope, his sonar device.

'Breathe deeply.'

She heaved, her bosom lurched. A teardrop fell from her left eye.

'No use crying.'

She bit her lip.

'X-ray?'

I gave him the cover. He placed it on a backlit board.

'Hmmm.'

He sounded clueless.

'Blood report?'

'All clear,' I said, handing him another cover.

Her coughing returned and went on for a while. She couldn't stop. The doctor stood, his shoulders slumped. He scratched his head.

'What does your husband do?'

'Which one?'

The doctor looked to me for help.

'The first was a benefactor, he is gone,' I said. 'The second was a painter.'

'Was he the artist you brought with you some years ago?'

'Yes.'

It had been a fruitless consultation.

'Hard of hearing, right?'

Amma nodded, not trusting her throat enough to speak to the ENT specialist. She remembered suspecting his credentials. He had strange questions.

'How does he paint if he cannot hear properly?'

She had laughed, tears streamed down her cheeks.

'What is so funny?'

She couldn't even begin to tell him.

'We are so helpless,' she said.

'Helpless?'

'I find the desperate funny.'

'I am sorry?' said the doctor.

'His eyesight is good,' she said.

'But tell me,' said the doctor, 'doesn't lack of hearing affect what he makes?'

Amma had spoken to me about her second husband, Ravi's father, an artist she had met by chance. She had described a visit to his studio, how she had climbed a narrow wooden staircase that opened into a ten by ten sunlit paradise. The painter was deaf, she had been told.

It could have been the harsh sunlight but she felt his colours were muted.

Maybe it was just her.

He painted portraits. Of people he met in passing, he said. He had a sharp eye, she thought, to be able to capture someone so well. The portraits were intriguing. The people he had painted were oblivious to onlookers, if at all they seemed to be searching within themselves. How did he do it? How did he make something so arresting that viewers couldn't help standing and staring?

There was a work on the easel that grabbed her attention. It showed an empty room, a man sat at a table, and time for some reason stood still. By his posture he wasn't waiting, not for anyone or for anything to happen. She stood and looked at it till her feet hurt. It taunted her, that work. It held some secret that she would never unlock, a truth that was perhaps the perfect lie.

'It was him, painting himself,' she said later. 'That stillness was his silence. I was moved to get to know him better, to change his life in some way. I tried.'

Ravi's father was of modest circumstance, a man who had barely managed to subsist, who was clearly a rare talent that deserved better, but the art world was fickle and refused to be democratic in its largesse. She sought him out, took him to the salon that mattered, secured the backing of a collector who was a Pied Piper in Mumbai. His work moved into rooms where the important gathered. Museums took notice and it was only then that she let up.

'We have an antique wall clock,' she told the doctor.

'And it tells time?'

'My husband says he can hear it.'

'I see.'

'In the meanwhile, I have started shouting at people.'

She began laughing again and this time the doctor smiled.

'Sometimes I don't understand my patients,' he said.

The Dictaphone was on. Amma began to ramble.

'On the other hand, some people were just what they were. You wished for more.'

Her third husband was peerless in his behaviour. He was a calamitous bore. Every social occasion unmasked him. In private, at home, there was no place to hide and she had seen the low limits of his intellect, the repetitive nature of his inquiry on life. The most prosaic future lay before him, dull as could be imagined.

'Let us say he was a man in a cocoon of his making. He would go to any lengths to protect that cocoon. What did we share? Ordinary moments, predictable days, everywhere a sameness.'

'What did you see in him, then?'

'I don't know,' she said.

'So what did you do?'

She had to engineer something, a life-affirming manoeuvre. She did so without hesitation, freed herself and sought the company of someone else. That someone else wasn't worth recording.

'Can you tell me more about Ravi's father? The painter.'

'Do you know that Ravi's father could speak? He was deaf but he spoke clearly. He sounded different.'

She cocked her head to a side as if she was listening to him.

'Tone-deaf,' she said. 'It sounds cruel but he was tone-deaf when he spoke.' After a while, 'He spoke a lot when he had had his two drinks. He would call me things, belittle me.'

'Why?'

She shrugged. 'I didn't mind his words. His tone was what I couldn't stand. It was monotonous.'

'Amma,' I said. 'A question.'

'What?'

'How come you made nothing of me?'

The question threw her.

'You?'

'Yes, me.'

She thought for a while.

'Why have children, Amma?'

'Kumara, you just happened,' she said.

She placed a hand over her mouth, a sign of regret?

'As did Ravi?'

'Ravi I wanted,' she said.

There was a silence that made her uncomfortable. 'I could have done better,' she said. 'Admittedly.'

It was too late, it was also pointless.

'You could do better, you know,' said Amma. 'But you are afraid.'

'Afraid of what?'

'I don't know. Confrontation perhaps. Complexity?'

'I have done very little that people will remember,' I said.

She scratched her head. 'You take simple decisions. I can predict them.'

It wasn't a compliment. I guessed at that moment who my father was.

'Life is too short, Kumara,' she said. 'I had my talent. I couldn't sit around and worry about you. Or Ravi for that matter.'

I did something bold after this conversation. I met my former boss who in many ways was a stranger to me. We got talking. Over a couple of hours, we spoke a lot about ourselves. I slipped into confession mode.

'I have no secrets worth revealing.'

'Hmmm,' he said.

'You know my career, it was predictable. I have nothing to hide.'

'You have never done anything regrettable?'

'No,' I said.

'You sound like you are full of regret.'

I invited him home for a bite. He had never been to my place. He liked it.

'A house that has interim spaces,' he said. 'Is this you?'

'My mother,' I said. 'This is her place.'

There was a porch, there were verandas, galleys and corridors. The kitchen was separate, a few steps down, a few steps up.

'This was also a dance school?'

'Yes. The dancers were all over the place. They are a communal lot. They would gather, sit on the floor, pose in doorways. They swayed when they walked.'

My boss walked around, stepping lightly.

'She is so famous,' he said, 'and this is her place. I must thank you.'

There were photographs on the walls, freeze frames from her performances. He moved from one to the other.

'Arresting,' he said. 'I can imagine what she must have been in full flow.'

'These are from another time, boss,' I said.

He saw the photographs on the mantelpiece.

'Were you married? Do you want to talk about that?'

My wife had walked away. Five years together and she said I dulled her senses. We had a sensible discussion and an amicable divorce. We meet up now and then. I like what she has become.

Months whizzed past us. Amma had trouble moving around on her own. She fell badly in the bathroom and broke her hip. She was bedridden for a while.

I called Ravi. 'When are you coming? It is time you took care of her.'

'I will come,' he said. He didn't say when.

'Why don't we sell the house?' I said. 'We need the money. I could do with some.'

'You asked her?'

'Not face to face. On the phone. She hung up.'

The topic irritated her. No discussion. She said later the house was precious. What was precious about it? Memories, she said. It didn't matter to her that she was stuck in a home and poor Kumara was struggling.

I kept looking at my phone, willing it to come to life. It rang as I was about to sleep. It was Ravi. His voice was faint, I could hear an onrushing wind.

'Machan?' he said.

'Are you out somewhere?'

'Yes. We are in a vineyard.' The phone crackled. 'You won't believe how old this vineyard is.'

'Like I care,' I said.

'Take a guess.'

'Eighty-nine?'

'You said it!'

That was our mother's age.

'How is she?' he asked.

He had the right to ask even if he hardly met her. He sent money you see, for maintenance, a kind of old age alimony.

'How is the wine?' I asked in turn.

'Haven't tasted it yet,' he said. 'We are doing the vineyard tour first, then we will go to the tasting room.'

'Nice,' I said.

There was so much my brother had to say about his obsession with wine. He called me often, usually after a tasting, in a mood to share his intelligent passion. I wasn't convinced there was anything more to wine than language that sought to obscure an addiction, which made a virtue of being dissolute. It did not help that invariably I would be in the home smelling lemongrass cleaning fluid, watching lonely, old people.

'I am standing next to a vine,' shouted Ravi. 'An old vine.'

'You don't have to shout,' I said.

'You should see it. It has a twisted trunk and gnarled branches. It is making faces at me.'

I had seen pictures of a vineyard. Orderly rows of shrubs, five feet high perhaps, green and leafy, on a gentle slope that stretched into the horizon.

'This is an old vine vineyard,' said my brother. 'It is very different. These vines are so rowdy!'

My brother, a dry chap, sounded like he was moved. 'Right now they have no leaves, leave alone fruit.'

'Sounds bleak,' I said.

'Yes,' he said, 'quite bleak. Imagine, smoke in the air, the land barren, some scattered vines, crooked and dark, and no people. It is like walking into an Anselm Kiefer painting.'

'What?' I said. 'You walked into what?'

'Nothing,' he said.

He carried on. 'Wine from these old buggers have such mystery, machan! So much character. It is hard to explain.' He tried explaining. 'Age-old vines produce small berries that are more intense. The wines have more structure.'

Next comes poetry, I thought.

'The winemaker here, he says these vines are niggardly with their yields and hard to harvest. But they are as precious as artefacts and they deserve our care.'

'Bro,' I said, 'I drink filter coffee, so spare me the gobbledygook.'

'I know, machan, I know. What do you call your coffee bean?'

'Arabica.'

'This wine is called Zinfandel. Isn't that a lovely name?'

'Yes,' I said.

I heard him sigh. 'The search for meaning ends with wine,' he said.

He spoke to someone. 'And these?' I could hear some laughter. 'I just asked about the oldest vine they have. It is their first planting and they still nurture it.' His voice dropped to a whisper. 'The winemaker is a soppy fellow, he is quite sentimental. He has given it a name.'

'I see,' I said.

'It's a she by the way. He calls her Zin.' His voice softened. 'I hope Zin survives this winter.'

'Deep down you have feelings, bro?' I asked.

He paused for a moment. 'Hey, are you trying to tell me something?'

He was sharp, my brother, and sensitive. 'Listen,' he said, 'you didn't tell me. How are you doing?'

'I am fine,' I said. 'I am just feeling a little out of sorts.'

My brother's voice softened some more. 'I am sorry,' he said. 'I know. I understand. Are you still there at the...'

'No,' I said. 'I left some time ago.'

We held the line for a few minutes. We had nothing much to say yet we let time pass by, let sounds filter in from around us. Finally, he spoke. 'Machan,' he said, 'should I send some money?'

The oversized medicine chest was fitted into a corner, where it jutted out and grazed hips. It was decades old, had irregular edges and three drawers that wouldn't open in winter. On top were two open shelves that held tablets, capsules, powders and ampoules in plastic packets and transparent boxes. In the drawers, there were files with scrawled prescriptions and some box files that held her test reports.

Nobody could touch that chest, not even me. She caught me staring at it.

'Story of my life,' she said.

'Yes, Amma.'

I was part of the story. I would accompany her to clinics and dispensaries, wait in queues with sick people, crying children, anxious parents fighting with each other. I would sit outside when she went in and had long discussions. She would emerge with prescriptions clutched to her chest.

'Ampoules to ampoules,' she once said. 'Drug to drug.'

Quite the drama queen. I looked at her, seated on the stuffed chair next to her bed, crooked spine, hunched shoulders.

'Don't pay for the last consultation,' she said. 'The elderly doctor kept quoting from the scriptures.'

'What?'

'He had the gall to say some things I just have to accept.'

She tried to straighten, she groaned.

'What will I do with this spasm? It comes and goes in waves.'

It was a frequent visitor, capricious and debilitating. I stood behind her, reached below and pressed a nerve. I knew where it hurt the most, the pain travelled down her legs.

She was grinding her teeth. 'Should I take the muscle relaxant?'

'Why not?'

'I lose bladder control.'

'Did you order the pads?'

'No.'

She balled up her fists. 'They are too bulky.'

She was staring at the wall. 'The days are getting longer,' she said. 'Things are so slow in the afternoon. I don't know what to do with myself.'

'Are you back to your reading?'

I had to change the topic. Her two friends at the home had passed away within a week and she had put away her books.

'The place has started echoing,' she said. 'It is so empty.'

The place was full, in fact, it had a long waiting list. Beds were at a premium.

Her eyes were slightly opaque, milky, as if a film was forming, and when she stared without blinking, it was scary.

'I am now officially the longest resident here.'

'Who told you?'

'The two owners. I don't know their names.'

I wished they hadn't.

'I feel they are counting my days.' Her head dropped.

'Rubbish,' I said.

She wiped her spectacles. Her skin was looking better. Her hair was brushed and combed. I could smell her hair oil.

'How is the new helper?'

'She is a trained nurse. I told them I don't need one. They said it doesn't matter. Of course, it does. They charge more for her.'

'They do!' I blurted.

The monthly statement had changed. The home kept raising its charges and we dared not complain.

'Did you get a job?' she asked me. 'Are you applying?'

'Yes,' I said. I was well past fifty and the last interviewer told me my resumé was flabby.

'How will you pay my bills? Did Ravi send any money?'

That hurt. It always came down to money and to Ravi, the saviour. We sat for a while without speaking. She held the hem of her gown and traced the embroidery.

'They have a pod called Sleep,' she said. 'People who have entered it have all died. You should complain to the authorities.'

I had seen the pod. It was a ventilator.

'I used to sleep so well.'

'Try pills,' I said.

'Okay.' She smoothed her bed sheet, caressing the folds. 'I must make friends again.'

'What about your neighbour?'

'That old man?'

I burst out laughing. 'Ma,' I said, 'you are old as well.'

'He is not just old, he is feeble. He doesn't talk, he can hardly see. And he smells. Why don't *you* go make friends with him? Go on.'

'I will,' I said. I went up to the old man, sat with him. After a few minutes, he looked in my direction and nodded. I spoke to him and he smiled. Half an hour went by.

My mother smiled when I returned. 'I am feeling better,' she said, holding my hand. 'I like what you did. There is nothing more precious than time and a few words.'

She showed me a prick on the inside of her elbow. 'Injection,' she said. 'Some new treatment for pain.'

'Who gave you that?'

'The owners.'

'Did you check with the doctor?'

She shrugged. 'I do what they say,' she said. 'We are afraid of them.'

'Why?'

She wouldn't say. I got up to leave. Even as I reached the door, she started weeping. I stood near the medicine chest feeling hollow and helpless. I wanted to break that damn thing, burn it, destroy each ampoule, each useless powder. I wanted to fiddle with her dosages. What was the worst that could happen?

I was light-headed when I left the home. The sun was out, the sky was blue. I stopped by at a modest eatery and sat like a zombie. What had I done?

I dawdled for an hour and ordered a second cup of coffee.

Funny things were happening. There was this sound in my ear. First I thought it was a ringing sound, then I realised it wasn't. It wasn't very loud, I looked around and clearly others couldn't hear it. Was it a warning? Or was it some sign of organ failure? Did organs sign off with such notice?

I was getting paranoid with all this happening.

Someone asked me if I was gay. I looked up at him and looked away. I did not say anything.

'Would you like a drink?' that someone said.

I was about to say no, then I thought, why not? What would happen, what could he possibly do? I wasn't that old, I could run. Or I could excuse myself, go to the toilet or something. What if he followed me?

'I don't know,' I said.

'You don't know what?'

'Anything.'

'Weirdo,' he said.

I went home, took small steps, I was jumpy. I was sweating, my hands were wet. I was in this state when the phone rang.

'Ravi?'

'Who else?' he said.

'I was expecting a call from the home,' I said.

He paused. 'You sound strange,' he said. 'Something happened?'

'Maybe,' I said.

This story received a special mention at the Galley Beggar Short Story Prize 2020–2021.

Looking for a God

We were watching a documentary on widows in Varanasi.

'In my generation, the husbands are older,' said my aunt. 'Some are ten years older.'

She fingered the glass bangles on her left hand. 'I got these at my wedding. I will break them one day.'

In films, it was a dramatic moment when the husband died. The wife screamed, smudged the vermillion on her forehead, then symbolically shattered her bangles.

'Your husband is a boy scout,' I said.

She smiled. 'People like him. He means well.'

Uncle was a permanent presence in my life. I grew up in their modest place.

'I need to colour my hair,' said my aunt. She was trimming her eyebrows. 'White hair is so unruly.' She turned my face away. 'Don't watch me, look at him; see how he bends.'

Uncle was crouched, tying his laces. He straightened. He waited till nothing happened. He walked away. He looked like somebody I had read about, no, someone I had seen in a school play. This was Raja Harishchandra, a man held together by self-esteem, fortified by righteousness.

His name is Kasturi. He is the father I never had. He will die shortly.

My aunt is Vasudha. Five feet four inches. Perfect teeth, no trouble in her knees. She looks graceful.

'I speak four languages—and you?'

She reads history, picks her films, listens to stalwarts like Chembai and Madurai Mani Iyer. She visits a small temple nearby. The priest, a portly man, chats with her. She goes late morning when the sanctum is shut. They sit under a tree.

I met her one day on her return. 'Vasu Aunty, are you looking for a God? I know a good one.'

She wasn't impressed. 'You are quoting someone?'

Their apartment in Nanganallur, a suburb in Chennai, had its share of Tamil brahmins, the less affluent ones. The colony had twenty-four buildings, four storeys tall, each with a stilt for parking. The settlement was classified as Middle Income Group. It took five years for the paint to peel, a few more for pipes to leak. Nanganallur brahmins had meagre habits. Their needs were modest. Mostly they needed money to satisfy the next generation. When the next generation got antsy, they borrowed.

There was a pawnbroker on the road to the temple. He took jewellery as collateral. The loan amount was less than half the assessed value. The interest rate was a flat 30 per cent, taken upfront. The terms were usurious. The pawnbroker, Bhagwat Tarachand, wore a white Gandhi cap, a kurta and a dhoti. He was an affable man who sat on a mattress, leaning on a round bolster. Behind him were portraits of deities. His son sat a step below, he lit incense sticks and the shop smelt of sandalwood. Tarachand knew the family histories of most people in the vicinity. He would greet them personally. Borrowers came in, hesitant and anxious, their jewellery wrapped in old cloth. If the material held up, junior would place it in a safe and count out the loan amount. Transactions were few, most days father and son drank tea and stared at a small television.

Kasturi was fascinated by this venture. He heard whispers of those who had borrowed. This kind of borrowing was considered desperate in his community. Kasturi asked for details from a chartered accountant. The chartered accountant, one Loganathan, explained the terms. Kasturi was aghast. 'Criminal, I say.'

'There is no statute against such lending,' said Loganathan. 'It is usurious but the principle of caveat emptor holds.'

'I have an idea,' said Kasturi.

He thought it was an original idea, a brainwave. Twenty would form a group. Every month, each would put up a hundred rupees, the kitty would have two thousand. The bidding would start. The highest bidder received the two thousand rupees, six months later the bidder had to pay up the bid amount which was distributed to the nineteen others.

'It is so simple,' said Kasturi. 'What can go wrong?'

'This has been done before,' said someone.

'Women call it kitty, men call it a chit scheme.'

'Let's try.'

They did. Soon, every month, the colony had five chits running. It spread. Kasturi gave it a name. He skimmed a small commission. The chit amounts increased to a level that made the chartered accountant distinctly nervous. 'This needs to be registered or something,' said Loganathan.

The monthly amount hit a crore, then two. It went to five and Kasturi lost control when people defaulted. A couple of really bad eggs left town.

Members who were restless with delays and excuses filed a cheating complaint. The absconders were away, the police questioned Kasturi. They came from a special cell. They came in a jeep.

'I have done nothing wrong.'

'There is a law governing this.'

'I told you,' said Loganathan.

'I was too caught up,' said Kasturi. 'I was doing a service. I was saving them from Bhagwat Tarachand.'

A meeting was convened where everybody gathered.

'There is a written complaint,' said the police. 'What should we do? There is a violation and there is a procedure against violators.'

They reached a friendly agreement. Nobody wanted Kasturi behind bars. 'Give me time,' he said. He looked mortified. To begin with, he refunded the commission he had received, a small amount. 'He is a good man at heart,' said someone. Vasudha was his wife, she was popular too. They gave him time.

The incident received coverage in a local paper. Somebody put up the cutting on the colony wall. Kasturi saw it, grimaced, and left for his native place in Thanjavur, ostensibly to sell some family land. He stayed away for six months. He brought back the money, not all of it, enough to placate people for a while.

'You think we have done enough?' asked Aunty.

Uncle and Aunty went around meeting the people who had lost money. Aunty was kind, hopelessly kind, and she shed the odd tear. Uncle said the same thing everywhere. 'I am sorry for your loss.'

'We considered shifting,' said Aunty. 'There wasn't enough money with us to make the move, and frankly, I could have done without the inconvenience.'

Kasturi had to face people, avoiding eye contact. He wore a cap and looked down when he walked. Unasked questions rang in his ears. The murmuring in corners hounded him. He did not say anything. He was quieter than before. The fun-loving senior had forgotten how to laugh.

'Are you embarrassed?'

'No, Uncle,' I said, 'I am not.'

He didn't like that. 'You should be.'

In time, Kasturi would die and go up in smoke, he would be reduced to ash in a pot. That pot would travel north to a temple town. In the meantime, they shifted to my place. I stayed in company accommodation, an old bungalow.

I remember the day they moved in. Kasturi took his luggage to their room and we did not see him for a few hours. My aunt and I sat in the portico. It was a derelict place in a distant suburb, washed by sunlight, ignored by everybody else.

What did the bungalow have to commend it?

A rough garden tended by the elements. No trimming was needed, no fertiliser, no planting. There was sand in the driveway. A large, rusted gate that creaked on its hinges. Dogs from the street hesitated near the entrance, sniffed the air and pissed on the side.

I liked the garden the way it was. There were flowers that spat pith, touch-me-nots, thorn bushes and nettles. There were butterflies and dragonflies, grasshoppers and the odd praying mantis.

'Some might call it ugly,' said Aunty.

'Why?'

'It is a little unruly.'

'What would you look for in a garden?'

She thought about it. 'A basket of sunshine,' she said.

I caught her writing a letter.

'A friend,' she said. 'A letter-writing friend.'

She saw the look on my face.

'Could you? Have a private correspondence in this day and age?'

I couldn't. I had nobody to write to, even if I did what would I write about? The idea of a personal correspondence felt odd.

She kept the letters in a wooden box. That box was on her dressing table, where I could see it.

I had to open the box at some point. I think the permission was tacit.

'You wrote to me,' she said, 'when you were in college.'

They supported me through college, my uncle and aunt. I must have written out of a sense of duty. Perhaps for money. And she had kept those letters.

I learnt her friend, the one she wrote to, was a poet. When a letter arrived, she would take a knife and slice the pasted end carefully. She had her seat in the garden where she would sit and pull out the sheet. She would take her time, savouring the words. From time to time, she would place the letter aside and be lost.

In the midst of her reverie, she would call out to me.

'Could you check on Kasturi?'

He was a shadow in the house. We saw him when the sun rose and set. We saw him lose weight, saw his eyes retreat. He lost his confidence.

'I have done wrong,' he kept saying. 'I am an accused, I say.'

Occasionally, he was incoherent.

My aunt tried to rationalise. 'How long can you harbour guilt?'

There was a sordid physicality to the dark misdeed. Kasturi received letters. Some were personal missives in the form of complaints. Some were pleas from older folk who were hurting. Some were threats that came by registered post. He got worked up when the postman rang the bell and insisted he sign the acknowledgement.

'Things aren't going well,' he said.

'With what?'

'My health.'

He lay in bed during the day staring at the ceiling. Aunty and I would knock and enter. His room would be dark, the curtains drawn, and there would be letters strewn on the floor.

'What is he doing, hiding in there?'

My aunt sighed. 'He is serving a sentence.'

We were helpless. I sensed a denouement.

Some work came up and I had to travel for a month. 'Go,' said my aunt when I hesitated. I was away a couple of weeks when Kasturi called. His voice was faint.

'I am having trouble with a few things. Can you come for a day or two? Please? If you can manage. I know you are busy.'

I returned in a hurry. I arrived breathless, hoping it wasn't something serious. He greeted me at the door. He looked fine, if anything a little better. When I looked askance, he came up with a few minor complaints. Trouble sleeping at night. Breathlessness climbing stairs.

'Why have you called me?' I asked.

He smiled. He looked happy and a little mischievous.

'I knew you would come.'

'Don't you do this again,' I said.

'Why? You won't come the next time? Is that it?'

We sat late into the night, had something to drink and we spoke a lot.

'Kanna,' he said, around midnight. 'The reason I called—the accumulated interest on the defaults has crossed the principal amount.'

And suddenly, he looked like the man I had left behind. I couldn't say anything to relieve his gloom. I left early the next morning before he awoke. I never saw him alive again.

A year after they shifted to my place, he took his life.

I returned once again. My aunt met me at the gate, she was bedraggled. 'I have tried everything.' She caught hold of my arm. 'Hurry!' She dragged me to his room. 'I massaged his chest, look.' He was there on the bed. 'He is not responding.'

He was long gone. He was cold by the time I arrived. I held him and it was disappointing. A cold body is nothing.

My aunt sat next to him, her eyes flowing. 'You were his son,' she said. She looked at me. 'You should have known.'

His will was read out. What remained to be apportioned was meagre. We had rummaged through his personal belongings, not sure what we were looking for. There was an old telephone directory. Expired driving licences, passports and a few bills. No property, no photographs, no stamp collection. There was an envelope. Short letters that were like messages, which he had not posted. They were heartfelt apologies.

For a long while, I had held this man up against the light and walked in his shadow. It hurt me when he fell short in measurable ways. I hoped I would in time forget him. This part of my life was better buried.

'You will remember,' said my aunt, divining my thoughts.

I looked at her with some affection. I was a little scared that she was ageing as well.

'Don't hide your hurt,' she said.

'I am not hurt.'

'Hurt isn't evil.'

'Fine,' I said.

'Hurt abates when you let go, truly let go.'

I couldn't.

On her insistence, I bought a notebook and started a diary.

Dear Diary

My aunt is seventy years old, she is a cheerful sort, in a good place in her own estimation. She is at an age where she is free to indulge, and she has moved from my house in Chennai to a one-room set in Mumbai that has 599 neighbours. She has a nest egg, she says, and it is safe in a bank bearing some interest. She wishes to travel and I—who have largely stayed put in Chennai, with a regular day job, one who is wedded to the crossword, long, aimless walks, conversations with shopkeepers and evenings at a frugal bar—am her chosen accomplice. She says we should be able to travel together despite everything. We had our disagreements. I remember a heated discussion on my difficulties with God, the need for representation and ritual, which she felt was important—pillars of belief she called them.

She wrote me a letter.

This is about Kasturi. I have a recurring dream. I wake up, rubbing my eyes, and he is there standing in my room. He parts the curtains, opens the dusty windows and cleans his spectacles. I wake up to find myself speaking to him. I am worried. I told somebody this is what is happening. She said, not to worry, it's just a dream. What if he replies, I said. She laughed. Then please consult a doctor, she said.

How are you, kanna? Please write to me.

I am getting used to Mumbai. This city wakes up late, unlike Chennai. Every morning I am alone, the rest are sleeping. I remember the weeks we stayed with you in your house, your garden. It was a difficult time, harsh and unforgiving. I remember how the evenings were long, Kasturi in the veranda, nursing a pale cup of tea. The moonlight confusing the dark, making shadows, contorting his slim frame into odd lengths.

Kanna, I need to travel. I need to get away.

Dear Diary,

My aunt's letters have made me aware of my situation. I am alone, I am having trouble passing time. Each day is long at the office, the weekends are interminable. I am tired of watching the news.

I have rediscovered music. I have a huge collection of CDs that Aunty used to rummage through. She has left most of the CDs in the wrong covers. I play whatever comes to hand.

I am so bored I examined my medicine chest. Most medications have expired. I found unused sunscreens and moisturisers. A few ointments of doubtful provenance. What I use regularly are plasters in different shapes and sizes. After many decades of use, my feet have worn out.

I was happy when Vasu Aunty called. 'Kanna,' she shouted, 'come with me to Varanasi before they change its name.'

She had been to Ajanta, Ellora, Khajuraho and Dwarka. Next on her list was Varanasi.

'A giant catchment area for people like me,' she said, on the phone. 'Please come and please bring him with you.'

She fixed dates, we found a place to stay, a yoga ashram in Assi Ghat run by Mr Purshottam, Purshottam ji as we began calling him. In the online world, he was a fair man wandering in his compound plucking flowers for the morning puja. According to posted reviews, his wife was in charge of the kitchen and the food was average.

Purshottam ji taught yoga and he had a local clientele. He was a man of few words.

'Breathe in to the count of six, hold for four, breathe out to the count of eight.'

His ashram was on the banks of the holy river and while this afforded a glorious view, there were a million mosquitos that buzzed in ears, settled on limbs and interfered with postures.

The ashram had two floors. Below was a dining space, the kitchen and a veranda in a horseshoe shape. It had folding chairs, a sagging charpoy, a table and some potted plants. Electricity came and went. On the first floor was a matching veranda for the yoga sessions and it was flanked by ten rooms. The rooms were modest, kept clean, two single beds each, an air conditioner, a bucket and a mug, a mirror and two windows. Mornings the sound of brushing teeth, evenings loud yawns, the toilet flush active for those who had eaten street food. The breakfast table was busy and it was where people met.

All this we learnt on the first day. My aunt does not snore nor do I, so we slept well. When we unpacked, our toiletries fought for space in the small washroom. Hers were quaint, she used brands that I thought had expired. I had my gadgets.

'Me first,' she told me the first morning. In she went before I could arise. I could hear everything. I stepped out into the corridor, walked to its end, and before me was Ganga Ma, an abridged version, the pre-monsoon one with flow having thinned, water having receded. It was still a postcard view. I killed a handful of mosquitos.

We descended for breakfast. Mrs Purshottam had hired a maharaj. This was a title given to gifted cooks. Her maharaj was upset he had no assistants. They quarrelled often over the menu (boring), the preparations (insipid) and his attitude. A peace was brokered. Everything was fried. Thankfully, good ghee was available in Varanasi.

'Puri and kachori for breakfast,' said the missus.

Aunty frowned. 'We are here for a week,' she said. 'One week of this and we will fall sick.'

She did fall sick.

The first two days, we walked the streets with an expensive tour guide. We saw fascinating temples, walked up and down ghats, met the poet Subramaniam Bharti's nephew—he was eighty years old, a sprightly, talkative gent, former professor of Banaras Hindu University. And we ate in many roadside eateries. We ate aloo kachori and drank pehelwan lassi.

While we stood at the roadside place with our lassi glasses, a chant reached our ears gathering strength seemingly with every step. We turned towards the sound. From a crossroads, a procession appeared marching in rhythm.

'Oh no,' Aunty whispered. 'Don't look.'

It was too late. Four men were carrying a body, a man carried a smoking pot ahead of them and two young men followed, their heads were shaven clean. They came.

Pitter-patter pitter-patter

'*Ram naam satya hai.*'

Pitter-patter pitter-patter

'*RAM NAAM SATYA HAI.*'

The procession moved past us, halting briefly for a vehicle.

'*Raam naam satya hai*,' said the lassiwala, slapping a wad of cream onto the curd.

'*Ram naam satya hai*,' said the next-door paanwala, folding betel leaves with one hand.

The procession faded, the street resumed its activities.

'You want to say something?'

'Yes,' said Vasu Aunty, clearly affected. 'Is this common? I mean I had heard about it, but still.'

Before she could say anything more there was another. Pitter-patter it went. *Ram naam satya hai*, they said. It was the route to the burning ghat and we were in the way. This time we stared.

'I saw the man's face,' said Aunty, a little overcome. 'Where do these people come from?'

'From far,' I said. 'They all do. Something calls out to them to make this final journey.'

'Look at us,' she said.

Yes, we too had an official reason.

'Where have you kept him?'

'In the cupboard,' I said.

'You don't mind sleeping with it?'

'I do. Last night I got the heebie-jeebies.'

She looked troubled. She pulled strands of her hair and tucked them behind her ears. She did this a few times. We walked aimlessly, a good way to discover the city. We came across a bhang stall. Government approved, said the board. Bhang came from cannabis. In this town of sadhus and sants, babas and bodies, aartis and cremations, bhang was perhaps the answer to difficult questions.

'I could use some,' said Vasu Aunty.

My stomach rumbled that night. Aunty spent all of it in the washroom, throwing up. The next morning, she was white and weak. She whispered. 'Nobody warned us.'

She ran a temperature the whole day and couldn't keep anything down.

'Is there a hospital nearby?'

A doctor arrived, summoned by Mrs Purushottam, and he took a look at her and administered an injection.

'Routine,' he said. 'I keep five ampoules in my bag at any time. Where did you eat?'

'I am dying,' said my aunt.

'You are in the right place,' the doctor laughed.

She took a day to recover and it was a miraculous recovery. She spent the day reading the travel brochures. 'So much useless information.'

She found something. 'Bookshop,' she said, her eyes bright. 'Called Harmony. It is right here in Assi Ghat.'

We went the next morning, wore slippers in a hurry and stumbled over the broken pavement, some steps that went hither and thither, two steep ones and then the road, pockmarked with dried cow dung. The store was a haven. We entered and music was playing.

'Rashid Khan?'

'Yes,' said the owner seated at the billing counter. He smiled and waited.

'Raag Yaman?'

'Of course.'

They bonded instantly. I strayed and ruffled up Hinduism, a well-stacked shelf. There were so many books, I had no idea it was such a busy field. They were big books, hardbound, with tantric covers.

'Play Bhairavi,' said Vasudha.

The owner rummaged. My aunt sighed. 'Lovely,' she said, 'just lovely.'

I stood next to the air conditioner while she browsed. The owner fixed us up with a good guide. Mr Pandey.

'Banaras needs worshippers,' said Pandey.

'Why?'

'There is a temple surplus,' he said.

'Ha ha,' said Aunty, 'every tree here is a temple.'

'There are so many old people,' I said. 'Really old.'

'People come here for their final days,' said our guide.

'I read about it,' said Aunty.

'There are many ashrams full of such people. They come here to die. Some of them pray that it happens sooner.'

'Bizarre,' said Aunty. 'I am a believer and all that but something like this?'

'You want to see one such ashram? You want to meet such people?'

'Yes,' said Aunty, to my surprise. 'I would like to meet them, talk to them.'

'And dissuade them?'

'Yes, if possible. They need to know nothing is inevitable. Unless you will it.'

I realised her connect. She had failed with Kasturi.

I held her hand with both of mine. 'Let's not go there,' I said.

Our young guide waited. My aunt relented. We continued our meanderings, my aunt was lost and hopelessly distracted. Pandey was a game trier, he had a sense of humour. 'These old people, I tell them, you stay in God's vicinity, why the hurry to meet him?'

'Rubbish,' said Vasu Aunty.

'Rubbish?' said Pandey. 'Ah yes, rubbish. It is part of the city's make-up.'

'Pandey!' I said. I had had enough.

'Huzoor?'

'*Raasta naapein?*'

We did get lost, though Pandey measured every step with a commentary to boot. Things sprang at us from street corners, narratives lurked in every stone. In quick succession, we saw a tree with a vermillion Hanuman, a sacred well, an old-style wrestling rink, Tulsidas's house with the Ramcharitmanas inscribed on the walls, a fertility temple and the rear view of the cremation ghats.

Our feet ached, my aunt looked for a place to sit. We thanked Pandey. He insisted on exchanging numbers. 'You will come back,' he said.

We walked down to a jetty. We hired a boat yet again and we went past the burning ghats, six to seven pyres lit at a time. Faint chanting drifted over the water, a sickly-sweet smell reached us, there was smoke in the air and the cries of tired relatives.

I decided I liked the river. A hired boat became a habit, we drifted aimlessly.

'You have come for tourism or you have come for punya?' asked one boatman.

Punya was a greedy word, it grabbed hold of neighbours like virtue, sacred, holy, auspicious and righteous, and ate up their meaning. Punya enslaved pilgrims for life. People journeyed without end, did yatra after yatra to sthal after sthal in their quest for punya. Varanasi, Haridwar, Amarnath, Vaishno Devi and Tirupati were sthals they went to.

'Why have we come?' I asked Aunty.

'I don't know,' she said. 'Kasturi never said anything about coming here. But I always wanted to. Sometimes you don't need a reason.'

That evening, she wasn't up to stepping out. I thought it was the stomach medicine and painkillers but it was probably her mind that was wrestling with a few questions.

'I will sleep it off,' she said.

She slept early, then tossed and turned. We woke up late the next day and we lazed in the ashram, wandered to a good view and took photographs. Pilgrims in boats with their reflection. They were singing. My aunt sighed, I smiled. Soon it was evening, our last, we hired a boat and set off to the ghats for an all-nighter. Our boatman, a small boy in middle school, rattled off the names of the ghats in good order. We floated past them, looking at the steps, the temples, minarets and alcoves. The river had lit candles placed on flowers. At Manikarnika Ghat, the pyres were burning.

'Don't look,' said the boy piloting the boat. We couldn't help looking.

'What's that smell?'

A foul smell hit us.

'Rotting flesh?'

'Pregnant woman or a cow,' said the young boy. 'They are not burnt. We release them into the river. Even infants. We don't burn infants.'

'Why?' asked Vasu Aunty, her eyebrows knitted.

I felt disoriented. Even Aunty looked upset. Her faith needed nourishment.

It arrived in a boat as we reached Dasaswamedh Ghat for the maha aarti. Two shaivites from the South, wearing the garb of priests and the emblem on forehead, rapped their temples with their knuckles, their wives in full nine-yard sarees sat next to them looking every inch like believers. One of the women had an exalted look on her upturned face, it was almost a performance. She was oblivious to her surroundings. I wish I could have captured that for posterity. She showed us what brought people from far and wide to Varanasi.

Gestures like hers moved me more than the theatre that Dasaswamedh Ghat provided. There was plenty of drama in the dark, large diyas with multiple flames, temple bells ringing, bhajans on speakers and young men rhythmically swaying in a cosmic dance, synchronised in their movements.

Aunty was still distracted and her lack of connect irritated me. The least she could do was... what?

At least look? Why come so far?

'You have his ashes?' She sounded anxious. 'You brought them?'

'Yes.' The pot was there on the boat, kept away where no one could see it.

'I am getting the heebie-jeebies,' she said.

It was late by the time the young boy found the perfect spot. Daylight wasn't far away when a pujari performed a puja. He chanted while we sat and looked at the water drift by. Nearby was a sadhu in orange, seated on the steps, his meagre belongings next to him. The sun rose slowly, light spread. It was quiet. The pujari nodded. I opened the cloth that covered the pot. Leaning over the side, I tilted the pot. Soft ash fell into the flowing water, some drifted in the breeze. After it emptied, I dropped the pot. It floated away. My aunt opened her eyes. 'Is it done?' I nodded. 'Then let's leave.'

The boat turned towards Assi Ghat, one last time towards the ashram.

'I don't know,' said Vasu Aunty. 'It felt so flat. Something was missing.'

I scratched my head. She shrugged and hugged her knees.

'Could be just me,' she said.

Over the softly lapping waves, we heard someone singing. It was an untrained voice, and the lilting melody came and went with the light wind. It drew closer. It was a boatman, he smiled as he sang his way past us. He sang with heart, he sang to the river, he sang to the skies. It was strangely moving. Vasu Aunty raised her face, her eyes were closed. She was in another world, listening.

'Breathe, Aunty,' I said. 'Don't forget to breathe. Inhale to the count of six, hold for four…'

'…exhale to the count of eight.'

She smiled, lowered her hand below the boat and caressed the water.

'Kanna,' she said, 'I am so confused. You asked once, I remember, about looking for a God.'

'Yes,' I said.

It was a poem by Arun Kolatkar. It was a good one.

An earlier version of this story titled 'I Believe' was one of the five commended stories in the Elizabeth Jolley Prize 2020.

Acknowledgements

The vacana of Allama Prabhu quoted in the story 'Long in the Tooth' was translated by A.K. Ramanujam in his book *Speaking of Siva*.

The Arun Kolatkar poem referred to in the story 'Looking for a God' is 'Yeshwant Rao'. You can look him up in the collection *Jejuri*.

Thanks are due to the team at Bloomsbury. This is my second book with them.

My agent, Priya Doraswamy, remains an amazing sounding board and helpful critic.

There are short story prizes overseas that have picked some of the stories in this collection. The judges are too many to name here but Monica Ali deserves mention for her wonderful Judge's Report for the Bridport Prize in 2018. An extract has been used, with permission, as a quote.

About the Author

After an MBA, V. Sanjay Kumar set up a finance company and a software enterprise, and in 1988, he partnered an art gallery called Sakshi. He began writing in 2010 at the age of fifty. In ten years as a full-time author, he has published four works of fiction. Cities inform his writing. A larger debt is due to artists, poets and musicians he has spent time with. *Ruffled Feathers*, his fifth book, has stories that have featured in award lists in the UK and Australia.